Shadows In Our Lives

A Collection of Short Stories

By

Thomas William Irons

This book is dedicated to my birth-mother,

Who chose life for me,

She became the first shadow in my life.

There are shadows all about you.

The noblest shadow is the one you cast.

Table of Contents

All In A Day's Labor 9

Saving the World 15

The Visit 25

The Tooth Fairy 37

The Shooter 45

Ray's Malt Shop 59

The Breakup 87

Richardson Park 101

Parody of A Home Coming 115

Norma Jean 119

Mud Lake 137

Going Home 163

Fletches Time 169

The Mystery of Curly Simmons 179

Corner Warriors 191

Afternoon Tea 219

A Sparrow's Song 229

All in A Day's Labor

You actually hear it before you see it, the sea. Its roar can be heard up on the path while you are moving through the shore pines. A primeval excitement stirs within, and you pick up the pace as you move down towards the beach. Your feet race, the heart pounds, the salt smell fills the nostrils and the dampness makes your skin feel moist. The sounds draw you as it has for a multitude of people throughout the ages.

Suddenly, the shoreline breaks into a panorama of ocean with white waves breaking on the beach sands. The strong sea-winds are blowing mist from the tops of the cresting waves and one sees the vapors moving out in an aerial display of color, a display that has been going on for billions and billions of generations.

On a clear, cloudless, morning you can look up and down the shoreline and see the tide either sliding-in or slowly retreating, depending on where you have entered the tidal cycle. Close your eyes.

If you listen closely, you will hear windy sounds of the past. And, if you listen carefully, you will hear the clatter of the future. A future that will be beyond your lifetime, but through the windy din you will know it as well as some future being who unwittingly will share it with you; sharing the future.

The waves have been coming up on this beach for countless eons; countless waves, constantly crashing down on the sands; countless waves, constantly beating the shoreline; countless waves, constantly altering it ever so slightly. Eroding and then rebuilding; depositing and then taking away. Creating and tearing down in a relentless symphony of subtle change. Clever and indirect, it's an evolution of change, of building, of destruction, and of perfecting—endlessly, eternally. Each wave brings with it something that will create a difference. Something that will be cause-and-effect, yet, when we look, we will see nothing.

The change is imperceptible, trivial and inconsequential. Nevertheless, it's there. It's there and if you look closely, measure precisely, observe critically, one can witness the change and Darwin will be appreciated.

Now, a participant comes across this relentless symphony, a Prince of the realm, a king of sorts. His kind has been part of the shoreline story for millions and millions of years. Thirty-three million years ago a fossil was formed that was found in recent times which proved his kind were from before antiquity.

They, too, have been changing, each generation, imperceptibly different from the last generation, each generation faintly grander than the previous. Each stronger, more equipped to survive and each more princely.

He is the perfect gull. Seagull, that is. It's a beautiful creature of evolution to be admired, appreciated, and treasured. This is a proud bird with clean white feathers that reflect back the bright sunlight to the point where it causes one's eyes to blink and look away for a second. His wings are hues of gray and black and spread out a couple feet when he is soaring above the shoreline scavenging for food. His strong, orange beak is long and bent down at its end, making it easier to pick up a morsel of food or hammer open a shell in which some creature is trying to hide. His webbed feet, also orange, are drawn-up underneath him as the Prince soars overhead taking in every inch of the shoreline, especially where the water flows to its highest point. It is here, at this precious apex, he will find the beaten up crab or the dead fish, which is offered up by the sea for his royal dinner.

For the last tens of millions of years, the hunting instincts of the princely gull have been polished to a fine point of perfection. He effortlessly catches the wind currents, gliding along, looking with yellow and green eyes that are precise and miss nothing. The eyes being able to spot the body of a dead crab the second it is thrown-up by the sea. As the tide recedes, the gull hovers over the corpse in anticipation of a meal.

But several Princes have spotted the offering. The only query now is which of the royals will claim the prize and as they hover.

Suddenly a handsome, large prince makes the claim by swooping in and grabbing the lifeless crab in his orange beak.

He grabs it on the fly, expertly snatching it from the sand as he glides a few inches above the wet. With it securely in his beak, he gains altitude, pumps his wings a couple of times, finds a current of wind and glides along the beach.

Now he is looking for a place to set the prize down. Its heavy and he will need to set the load down soon, break the shell and pull the morsel out.

Meanwhile, the Prince of princes decision has made the rest of the royal court continue up the coastline in search of another washed up offering. Occasionally they look back to make sure the prize hasn't been fumbled.

The winning Royal continues looking for a safe place to set the crab body down. A place safe from other royals, one's who would try to steal the prize. And, also, safe from those strange, four-legged barking beasts that walk with those bizarre, upright beings that have recently been strolling the coastal sands.

It is natural for others to want the prize. Someday, a younger, stronger prince will take the prize at will, but not today. This is his time, his day and no other is fast enough, strong enough, or big enough to take this prize. Today, the prize is his.

Finding a place free from people and dogs, the princely gull drops the crab shell and swoops in right as it hits the wet sand. Using his beak, he chops at the part of the body where the legs are joined. Here he will attempt to break the shell and pull out the crab. He is working hard to get at the morsels of meat, not noticing the other gulls have flown back and are circling overhead. They suspect trouble.

They come up the beach, two combers, each with a four-legged beast which is as corpulent as each of them. One is the mother comber, the other a dull looking son. Both wear sullen gray woolen clothes that keep them from experiencing the sea breeze and the clean refreshing feel of the mist. Each looks like they may bulge out of their tight sweats at any second. They each have thick, black rimmed glasses with lens that look as if they were made from bottle bottoms.

On their heads are straw hats and the wind has blown the rims flat against the hat crowns. One hat has a flashy, multi-colored band; the other has a white feather that is graying towards the end of it. Each is banishing a cane-like piece of driftwood that they had found a couple of mornings ago. The plump mother is poking around the sand looking for shells or sand dollars, looking almost like a blind person with a red and white cane.

The mother, walking just ahead of the dim-witted son, points here and there with her driftwood cane trying to tell him the secrets of the deep.

"Ah! Look, Jason, a 'baloney shell.'" And, "look, sand dollars. Almost perfect," she says with authority, and then unwittingly pokes it with her cane, breaking it into a hundred smaller pieces. "Oops! Wasn't all that great," she justifies. "Let's look for a better one."

Jason gives a bored sigh and then follows her up the beach. He's wondering why they are here? It's cold, and windy, and wet. Not much to do, either, he is thinking. What a waste!

Meanwhile, Mom has found another shell. She is bent over it trying to identify it with no luck. Again, she pokes at it with her cane and then flips it back into the ocean not realizing that it was a royal meal for the Prince of the realm she chased-off. His Highness hangs in the air, hoping the ignorant human will walk on before the ocean re-claims the dead crab.

Jason asks, "Why was that gull trying to tear it open?"

He is standing close to his lardy mother for warmth and through his thick glasses watches while she again flips the dead crab towards the surf. The podgy mother watches as the broken crab flies through the air and crashes into the receding wake.

As she watches, she sees the gull hovering above and with wild waves of her cane at him, "Get," she cries. "You'll not hurt this shell fish." She then grabs Jason and jerks him up the beach, proud that she has saved a living thing from such a creature.

The princely gull in all his finery merely adjusts his altitude higher and observes what has happened to his dinner. Then he looks to the two combers in their plebian garments walking up the beach, the larger one pulling the smaller and waving a stick. Her demeanor tells all that she thinks she has done something valuable.

The Prince turns gracefully, takes one last look at where the crab landed and then heads up the beach to rejoin the royal court looking for other dead morsels, just as they have done for millions and millions and millions of eons.

Saving The World

It not a long drive. Nor is it a tiring drive. The Naches Valley is stretched out from East to West for about twenty-five miles. It starts at the west-end of Yakima and meanders to the west about three miles past it namesake city, Naches. The Valley is divided almost in half by state Highway 12 and, surprisingly, has only two traffic signals, one at Highway 12 and the Old Naches Highway and the other in the little city of Naches. Actually, the traffic light is located on the south fringes of the city. If you leave Naches and drive East at sixty miles per hour you can pretty much make it to Yakima in about fifteen or twenty minutes; unless, of course, something happens to you on the way. This did befall Patti Henderfield, EMT, one, windy day in March.

It was the first day that she was a full-fledged EMT; an Emergency Medical Technician. And, because of her new title, she was out to save the world. On the seat next to her was her EMT First Aid Kit. A professional one, she had purchased with her own money and it had everything she needed for any type of emergency she might come across. She was ready! She was alert! She was an EMT!

On this March day, she drove East on Highway 12 heading toward Yakima and her first real assignment. She would be the EMT on one of the ambulance service trucks that served the greater Yakima area. Riding one of the rigs was not new to her because she had done this as a trainee. But, now, she would be the EMT, the one that would work with the paramedic. And, that was her next goal; to become a paramedic and save even more lives.

As she was driving, her mind went back to the day that she decided she wanted to be a medic. It was the day when a little three-year old girl got loose from her mom and ran out into the street. The driver of the car didn't have time to stop and ran over the little girl with golden blonde hair. Patti had been at recess when this happened and was going into the fifth grade building of Wilson Elementary. When she heard the screeching of the tires and looked over towards them, she saw the car run over the little girl.

Instinctively, she began to run towards the accident until she was stopped by the school fence. She watched as people milled around, most wondered what to do. Finally one person yelled to call 911. Then, someone else got a blanket and stooped by the little victim putting the blanket across her in an attempt to keep her warm and prevent her from going into shock.

The sirens were faint at first but then they became louder and louder, the wail and then a horn blowing and another wail. The large red truck pulled up next to where the girl lay. Two firemen jumped off the truck, one went directly to the little girl who was unconscious on the roadway. The other firefighter went to the back of the truck, opened up a door, and took out what looked to be a large tool kit.

Soon both the firemen were working on the little girl while a third fireman was directing traffic. More sirens were wailing and soon two police cars showed up and began to help with controlling traffic. An ambulance also pulled up and the two medics in their crisp white uniform shirts got out of the cab and immediately went to the back of the vehicle to remove a stretcher. They rolled it over to where the victim was being attended to by the firemen.

A small crowd had gathered behind the school fence and along the street. A woman in an apron who appeared to be the little girl's mother was crying and talking to the police. The medics had placed the little girl on the stretcher and were loading her into the ambulance. They drove away with the siren blaring and Patti saw the mother get into the police car still crying.

"Patti, it's late," Mr. Coleman, her teacher said, interrupting her thoughts. "You need to get to class."

Patti looked at Mr. Coleman and said with determination, "I'm going to be a medic some day." Then she turned and started running to her class.

Now years later, Patti remembered that day knowing it had been a defining moment for her. She had worked every minute of her life to become one of those medics she witnessed that day. They had worked hard to save the little girl. Only, now that she is a medic, her patients would always live because she knew she was the best. She could hardly wait for her first call as she continued to drive the length of the Valley towards her initial assignment.

The Naches Valley is a pretty valley with a river that meanders down the south-side. It's kind of tucked in under the Old Naches Highway and graceful old Willows grow every few hundred yards along the riverbank. Cotton Wood trees are all along the river, too. Some have collapsed in to the river current and others have become bridges that the farmer's children and animals use to cross over to the other bank. The under growth along the river is home to countless animals, snakes and birds, dogs and lots of wild cats and more homeless people than the county would like to admit. The homeless make campfires and their smoke is seen for miles on a calm, clear day.

From the homes on top of the East hills bordering the valley, you can see the entire valley's floor with its bright greens and browns. Beyond the valley, one can see the Cascades from up there on the ridge, which look purple and appear to be much closer than they actually are. Young people are always leaving the Valley, yet, by thirty-something they return because there is a mysteries hold this area has on its residents. Most return and stay for the rest of their lives.

The old highway follows the contours of the hills and it borders the valley giving it the texture of quiet country scene with a calm, smooth flowing river. The river provides life-giving water for trees, and animals, and farmers, each working to forge out a living in this beautiful valley.

White people have lived here since 1856 when the first settlers put up a fence. Indians of the Nez Perz tribe have inhabited the valley for thousands of years and the area around Naches was a principal meeting area for an annual powwow. History has recorded few clashes between the white man and the Indians in this area. They have tolerated each other and learned how to live together. The real truth is most of the Indians moved into the lower Yakima valley and thought the white man crazy for growing something he called apples.

A March wind was blowing across the highway, enough to stir up some dust and leaves. The wind was dry and comes down on the highway blowing in from the South. Out in the distance, Patti could see the leaves sweeping across the road and she could feel it push her SUV as it gusted in strong spurts. She was fighting the wind when suddenly she saw something. Not real defined yet, but she knew instantly it was some kind of animal in distress. It lay close to the highway edge but in her lane of travel. "Oh, God," she thought, "it's a cat. A cat, that's been hit by a car."

"Why can't people be more careful," she said out loud to herself, angrily. She started to slow down.

In that instant, she thought of her own cat, Max. He was a great cat with a real personality. Yes, he was needy and stand-offish all at the same time. But, she loved him dearly and would never dream of fixing something in the kitchen without him laying up on one of the side boards watching and waiting. Waiting for the inevitable morsel of food, she would give him. Yes, he was fat. A big, fat gray, loveable cat with stripes of black; he looked like a gray tiger.

"Who would hit a cat and then leave it lying in the street?" she said aloud. "What a jerk."

She looked again at the cat in the roadway and saw it jerking its head back and forth, almost in rhythm with the wind. It was a light tan and brownish with darker areas, almost black areas. She couldn't tell because the morning sun was bright and blinding. However, she knew she could save this cat. She was an EMT and working on a cat would be similar to working on a person who was hit by a car. At worse, she could put the injured animal in the back and drive it to the vets. She remembered there was vet just after she turns off the highway. "I hope I'm not too late," she said out loud.

Patti slowed down even more and was thankful that traffic was light this morning. It would be safer for her and the little victim. The head continued to bob in the wind. Patti was going over in her own head what she had learned in her EMT class about coming upon an accident site.

She checked her review mirror to make sure no one was following to close. She looked around the area to make sure no one else was involved in the accident. Expertly, she brought her vehicle to a stop right at the victim site, engaged her flashers and checked for any other vehicles once again. She glanced at the victim once more as she reached for her first-aid kit.

The wind was blowing a little harder and the cat's head was bobbing even more, like its pain had increased and it was in more distress. She needed to move, and to move quickly if she was going to save this victim. Carefully, she again checked for other moving vehicles, seeing none she flung her door open and jumped out with her first-aid kit in hand.

* * * * *

A couple of days earlier a young paper boy had been in the back of his father's Ford pickup folding papers and putting a rubber band about each one and then flipping them into a pile back towards the tailgate. Accidentally, one of the papers got caught by the wind and flew over the tailgate and on to the highway. "Damn," the farmer's son thought at the time, then without hesitation went on folding more papers, glad his dad hadn't seen.

The folded paper landed in the middle of the highway and came to rest in the number one lane, the fast lane. It laid there in the sun for quite a time before an eighteen wheeler roared over it causing it to take flight and then land right where a set of the truck's duals could run over it again, and they did. It caused the paper to bend and twist and take on an odd shape. When it landed, it landed in the number two lane right next to the outer lane single white stripe. There it lay for the next two days with the bright, hot sun drying it out, turning it a brownish yellow. Countless cars and trucks went by, none touched the paper. The way it was situated on the highway one could almost swear that it looked a bit like . . . well, a brown or yellow cat. Strange what can happen out on the open highway, in the heat and the wind?

* * * * *

Patti was just kind of frozen there, in place, looking at the two-day old folded newspaper. "Where's the cat," she thought to herself as she slowly walked up to the paper. One corner of the newspaper was flapping back and forth, kind of like a cat flicks its ear back and forth.

"Oh, my God!" she exclaimed. "What the hell have I done?"

She stood there over the newspaper with her professional EMT kit watching the uneven edge flick back and forth. The breeze that made the newspaper edge riffle now caught a slice of Patti's hair and flung it across her face. With a free hand, she grabbed the irritating hair and intended to flipped it back over her shoulder but the wind caught it again, just as she released it and it blew right back across her face as she stared down at the scorched newspaper.

Right about then a passing motorist slowed down enough and yelled out his passenger window, "Do you need some help?"

"No," replied Patti, thinking fast as to what to do. "I'm an EMT with first aid training. I'll take care of this situation."

"O.K. madam," he called out through the window. He looked down at the newspaper and added, "Had a yellow cat like that once." Then he floored his pedal, caught a little rubber, and disappeared down the highway.

Patti watched him as he drove off quickly. Now she moved quickly before any other good Samaritans decided to stop. Laying open her first aid kit, she knelt down next to the "victim" and imagined it was real. She checked for a pulse and broken bones.

"I better get you to my vehicle quickly," she said out loud. Her embarrassment was complete but she wasn't going to let it get any worse. She would pick up the "victim" and hustle it into her back seat and drive off like she was on an emergency run to the nearest veterinarian's office.

She reached into her first aid box and brought out a towel to place over the "victim," then she quickly but expertly lifted the "victim" off the pavement and turned to move promptly to her vehicle. This had to be done with alacrity and smoothly in order that any on-lookers would say she really knows her business.

Quickly she rounded the front-end of her vehicle, kind of turning wide and into the on-coming lane. She didn't see or hear the three-quarter ton, four-wheel drive truck with it big wheels making a loud whining road sound that big off-road tires make. She was too busy attending to her first real "victim." She knew her business and she was busy saving the world.

Patti may have realized at the last moment that she had made a huge mistake; not about the newspaper looking like a cat, but about the three-quarter ton truck that was just about to sideswipe her.

The drive tried to swerve out of her way but she had come around the front-end of her vehicle so fast that he could not react quick enough. The front bumper of his Dodge Hemi caught her right arm and elbow. It turned her so quickly that it broke her neck and threw her up against her vehicle. Then she bounced back into the speeding truck, which dragged her down the road for several hundred yards.

The drive yelled, "Get the fuck out've the way, Bitch!" as he pulled the steering wheel to the left and jammed on his bakes.

His passenger yelled, "Shit, Jesse, watch out!"

"Where in hell did she come from, George?" Jesse yelled as he set the brake and climbed down from the cab.

"Hell, I don't know Jesse," George replied. "Fuckin' bitch came out of nowhere. Carrying an animal or some'ton. Might 'a been some kind've cat."

Patti was laying at the edge of the number two lane when George and Jessi reached her. She didn't move, didn't make a sound. Jesse squatted down next to her and brushed back the hair that the breeze had blown across her face. He saw a small trickle of blood come out her nose and her eyes were open.

"Oh, God, Jesse, isn't she 'a OK?" George asked.

Jesse placed his hand on her neck to see if he could feel a pulse but felt nothing.

"Don't know, George." He tried her wrist and waited a moment before he said, "I'm a thinking she's a goner. Better call 911."

"911, how can I help you?" the operator said clearly.

Jesse was nervous but said, "A woman just run out on to the highway and I hit her with my truck. She acts like she's dead."

"What is your location?" the 911-call taker asked.

"We're on Highway 12, about three miles west from town."

"Town? What's the name of the town?"

"Yakima! About three miles out. We're headed to Yakima. You need to hurry," Jesse said as he looked down at Patti. "I think she's dead."

"What makes you think she's dead?" the operator asked.

Jesse, quickly explained how he check for her pulse just like they trained them to do when he took a first aid course for his farm work.

"And, I don't see her breathing," he yelled. "Just get us some help!"

George had been walking around the scene and could find no animal or cat anywhere. He thought that strange and said so to Jesse,

"Jesse, can't find the cat. Just some old'en newspaper wrapped in a small rag."

As the operator told Jesse to calm down, faint sirens could be heard in the distance. He had walked back to the front of her vehicle and could see the first aid kit. He told the operator what he saw and said, "Looks like some kind've first aid kit."

The operator said that help was almost there, as the sirens grew louder and louder.

"Can't figur'n who's she's a help'n," George said to Jesse. They were both standing there looking around when the ambulance drove up.

The first medic jumped out of the driver's side, went straight to victim, and looked at her. He stopped a moment as he recognized her, then he felt her neck for a pulse, which was absent. He looked up as his partner appeared pushing the stretcher and said, "Well, now we know why Patti's late."

THE VISIT

"Grandma, where do you go when you die?" Patrick asked while sitting in his car seat.

Mary, Patrick's great-grandmother, thought for a minute, then replied, "Well, Patrick, people like your grandfather go to Heaven where they can watch over those they love."

"What's Heaven, Grandma?"

"Heaven is a special place God made for people who are good and to go to when they die," Mary replied. "You go there for eternity."

"What's ternity?"Patrick asked bewildered, not able to pronounce the word.

"Eternity, it means forever, Patrick, forever," she replied, thinking, do they ever quit asking questions?"

"Oh," was Patrick's reply as he was trying to comprehend forever.

"Wow, is that a long time, Grandma?" He sat a moment then began to squirm and looked at the back of Grandma's head. "Is Grandpa watching us right now?" Patrick asked with some hopefulness. "Does he see us?"

"Yes, he can see us."

Great-grandma hopes this will satisfy Patrick's curiosity as they drive out to West Hills Cemetery. Patrick, seated in the backseat in his booster chair, had his seat belt securely fastened. As they drove, he looked at the trees and low-rolling hills that surrounded the valley. The traffic was light and Grandma Mary was having a good day considering her seventy-one years and four TSI's, none of which seemed to have left her with permanent damage.

"Are we there, yet, Grandma?" Patrick asked as he squirmed around in his seat.

"No, Patrick, we still have a little ways to go," replied Great-grandma. "Stay in your seat! Do you have to go potty?"

"Yes," Patrick answered. He suddenly ached with need, adding "Really bad!" Squirming more and clutching himself tightly, he could hardly hold from wetting his pants, but he was making a valiant effort.

"Well, we are almost there. Try to hold it," she encouraged him, but secretly hoped for a bathroom soon.

The road that leads to West Hills is a country road, two lanes, white line down the middle with cross streets every mile or so. The crossroads are usually unpaved and dusty, leading to a group of farm buildings a mile or two off the highway. There is one stoplight on the way, a four-way intersection that has a convenience store and a sign that announces "Public Restrooms." Mary saw the sign and breathed a sigh of relief.

"Patrick, do you want to stop here," Grandma asks. "They have a bathroom."

"Yes, grandma, hurry," squirming around in his car seat and clutching his pants. Then he asks, "Grandma, do you think Grandpa knows we are on our way to visit him?"

"Yes, Patrick," she replies dryly. "I think he does."

Great-grandma comes around to the back passenger side-door as Patrick bounds out of the car almost knocking her over. He is a tall boy for his age, blond hair, and brown eyes with constant curiosity about his surroundings.

"Patrick, slow down! You almost knocked grandma over," Mary says while trying to maintain her balance.

"I really have to go, grandma." Then he quickly adds, "Hurry, grandma! Hurry!"

"Patrick, take my hand," commands Great-grandma. "You don't run across parking lots."

"But I have to go!"

With grandma in tow, Patrick pulls her into the convenience store where grandma finds the door to the Men's room. She opens the door for Patrick and she is relieved that no one else is using the restroom.

"Patrick. Patrick!" she says loudly to get his attention. "When you're finished be sure to wash your hands."

"O.K. Grandma, I will," Patrick replies after she gets his attention away from the toy rack, next to the door of the restroom.

He dashes in and looks for the urinal, which is a bit high for him to reach. Pulling his zipper down and unbuttoning his pants, he gets on his toes as he manages to accomplish his mission.

While trying to tuck his shirt back in his pants an obese, filthy man enters who is either a ranch hand or homeless. He is dirty, smells, and is unshaven. A tattered, dirty red shirt barely covers his huge stomach and his arms seem too short. His dirty baseball hat is on backwards and covers graying, oily hair. He has a face rutted with deep lines that have endured a life of drinking, and smoking, and abuse. He has deep penetrating eyes that are cold blue, that look through everyone. He trusts no one, but he likes little boys.

"Hi," Patrick says, looking up at the man as he is pulling up his pants and trying to tuck his shirt. "I'm going to visit my Grandpa."

The loathsome man looks at Patrick and smiles, asking, "Are you alone, little boy?"

Sensing something strange, Patrick answers, "No, I'm with my Grandma. We are going to visit my Grandpa." He continues to struggle with his shirt; he cannot get it inside his jeans and button his pants, too.

The fat man stands there, his short arms hanging at his sides; he breathes in deep and loud breaths. He is a panting animal. He's staring at the little boy. He wonders if that elderly woman outside the door is the grandmother.

His eyes narrow, he looks quickly around noting that he is standing between the little boy and the exit. "Perfect," he thinks.

"Go back in the stall, little boy," he says with cunning. "I can help you there." His eyes focus on Patrick and a thin line of sweat begins to appear on his cruel upper lip as his breathing comes more often and deeper. Like a snake about to strike, his attention is focused. He is alert, not taking his eyes off his prey.

Patrick looks into the face of the man offering help as he continues to struggle with his jeans and shirt. "Dad is always saying the shirt should go inside the pants, but it's hard to do," Patrick thinks out-loud to himself.

"Could you help me," Patrick asks the man in desperation? Then as the man begins to step forward and reaches for Patrick's wrist, Patrick suddenly thinks what Dad has said about strangers! Like a bolt of lightning, Patrick kicks the hovering man between the legs and bolts around him for the door.

Mary, outside the men's restroom door, has been wondering what is taking her grandson so long. She didn't like the looks of that fat man in the red shirt. She wonders if she should call in through the door. Just as she reaches for the door, the door flies open with a loud BANG. Patrick comes tripping out, still trying to button his pants. He trips over the threshold and stumbles out into the customer isle, coming to his feet in front of the pop machine.

"Grandma, I can't ... this buttoned," he says with frustration. He stands there while she tucks his shirt and buttons his pants. Both are oblivious to the loud groaning and swearing in the men's room.

"I'm thirsty," Patrick states!

"Do you want Grandma to get you some juice," Mary asks.

"I want a Pepsi," Patrick demands.

"It's too early, Patrick," Grandma replies.

"Sometimes, Daddy lets me have a Pepsi early when we go fishing," Patrick fabricates. He goes to the cooler and helps himself to a can of Pepsi.

"O.K., Patrick," Grandma replied. "No, don't open it until we pay for it. Come over here, so I can pay for it. Stand still!"

As the middle-aged clerk takes the money for the Pepsi, Patrick opens the can, saying to the clerk, "We're going to visit my grandfather. He's dead, you know!"

"He's dead?" The clerk repeats, looking at Mary with a questioning frown, then remembers that West Hills Cemetery is just down the road a bit. He looks at Patrick, "Really."

"Oh, yes. And, he knows we're coming," Patrick remarks, then adds, "I miss him a lot." He says this following great-grandma out the door.

The clerk smiles to himself, watching Grandma and Grandson get in their car. He then turns his attention to a man with a quart of Pepsi, who is wearing a tattered red shirt.

"Anything else, Sam?

* * * *

West Hills Cemetery is located twenty miles west of downtown Yakima. Yakima is itself located in the Yakima

Valley, a valley noted for its Red Delicious Apples and wonderful flat land farming. It has a huge migrant worker population of illegal aliens that stream across the border from Mexico to find jobs in Norte Americano. They work their way through Texas picking local farm crops, then move on to California to work the tomato fields. Finally, they move up the coast and extend inland into the Yakima Valley, working the fruit orchards. Many have begun to stay and make the Valley their home. Hard workers, they ask for nothing more than to provide for their families. The wives work long hours in low paying jobs of restaurants, motels, hotels and in the agricultural industry.

The Mexican men are everywhere picking, harvesting, mowing lawns, painting, whatever tasks will provide for a family of several children and a wife. They live mainly on the Eastside of town. Because of this population, white flight has occurred. The white population is diligently relocating to West Valley.

The cemetery, perfectly positioned to receive this movement, will in future years enjoy prosperity and growth. It is the only cemetery on the Westside. To its credit it has a memorial section named Fallen Heroes, which includes war veterans, firefighters, police officers and other first responders.

"Well, Patrick," says Great-grandma. "We're here."

Patrick looks around at the new cemetery and its young evergreen trees and beautiful willows, which are neatly trimmed up off the ground by the resident gardener. To Patrick, they look like large umbrellas.

"I have to go potty!" he states out-loud as Grandma gives a gentle sigh.

"Well, it's that Pepsi," Grandma replies. "It's no wonder. Let's stop here at the office and ask if there is a restroom."

"Oh, yes. There on the left. Down the hall," points a prudish woman dressed in a gray pantsuit with a white blouse and black shoes. She is anticipating a funeral cortege to arrive any moment and acts distracted. She looks at the elderly woman and the young boy, who must be the woman's grandson. As the boy goes down the hall and finds the correct door, she thinks, "Grandpa must have died recently."

"Are you visiting, today?" She asks Mary.

"Yes, my husband," Mary replies, adding, "He is, or was, his great-grandfather." She indicates Patrick as he lets the bathroom door close behind him with a slam. "He misses his grandfather, so I brought him for a visit."

"Yes, it's hard on the very young," the funeral lady replies. "But, how are you doing, dear?"

"Oh, just fine," Mary replies, feeling the loneliness over take her as she speaks. "It just takes time."

"Yes, yes it does," she states. "Do keep yourself busy. It helps."

"Oh, I do. I am cleaning out Tom's closet and taking his clothes to the Goodwill. I am going to have a garage sale and then sell the house. I found a wonderful mobile home at the Golden Villa Park." With conviction in her voice, she adds, "And, there are a lot of senior citizens living there."

"When did your husband pass, my Dear?"
Mary replies, "Last September." She is bent over, buttoning Patrick's pants. He has just returned from the bathroom.

"Well, dear, don't move too quickly. Give yourself, and your family, a little time," she says gently. "Moving too quickly might be risky. Maybe a trip would do you some good, first. You know, before you sell the house."

"Oh, I'm way too, too busy for a trip right now," as she finishes helping Patrick.

"Can we go, Grandma," Patrick asks as he looks at the strange woman. "We going to visit my Grandpa," he adds as he continues to stare at the funeral lady.

"Yes, that's what your grandmother said," she replies, with a sympathetic smile. "Have a good visit!" With that, she hurries off to answer a phone that's ringing in one of the offices.

* * * *

From the Cemetery Office to the Veteran's Memorial section, it's a short walk. A picturesque stream meanders alongside a pathway lined with Thunder Plums that are displaying their pink flowers, each tree looking like a large pink cloud, making the path feel serene and tranquil. Their fragrance fills the air and the gentle breeze scatters the petals across the lawn and into the current of the stream. The pink flowers will soon be all gone as the spring season passes quickly and the trees dark maroon leaves begin to unfold and cover the pathway.

People stop and sit under the trees on the benches provided, to think and contemplate their losses, and their own lives. They think of their loved ones, who have passed into history, who have become embellished memories, who have become justification for a tearful cry, now and during holidays.

In the Fallen Heroes section are those men and women who fought WWII. Thomas Southerland was one of those soldiers. He fought the Nazi menace in Africa, then on to Italy, landing in Sicily and marching up the boot to Rome. He was the typical American GI of WWII who loved his country, loved his wife, loved his family and wanted nothing more than to get home safely.

His tastes, as was his life, were simple. He returned from the war and became a teacher. His life as an educator was uneventful, yet, his shadow touched many lives. He married Mary whom he had met before being shipped to North Africa and Italy. After the war they together raised four children and their marriage endured for fifty-four years.

Thomas died at home in his eighty-fourth year from a heart worn out by the years. As was his life, his death was orderly and well planned. Mary was well provided by his estate and he had a special and close relationship with his great-grandson Patrick. They often played Lagos together and when he passed, those same Lagos went to his great-grandson.

"This is it, Patrick," Grandma said. "This is Grandpa's grave. They haven't got his headstone, yet?"

"What's that say, Grandma?" Patrick asked, while pointing to the plastic, yellow marker.

"It's grandpa's name. Thomas Southerland," Grandma replied proudly. She pronounces her husband's name with extra force. And, then adds, "It's just temporary. I wish his headstone would get here."

"So, where is Grandpa?" Patrick looks around half expecting to see his grandfather, wondering when he will appear.

"Well, Patrick, he's in the ground. Buried. He's under the headstone."

"But you said the headstone isn't here"

"Yes, yes. I know. This is the temporary headstone." She points to the temporary plastic marker.

Patrick points to the marker, asking, "Is Grandpa down there?" The puzzled look on his face makes Grandma uncomfortable because she can't seem to find the right words to satisfy Patrick's curiosity. She never has had Thomas's patience and right now Patrick was sorely trying her.

"Patrick, what did grandma just say? Great-Grandpa is buried in the ground."

She begins to cry as Patrick falls to his knees in front of the marker. He bends his face close to the ground, then asks with confusion, "He's under the marker?"

"Grandpa!" he suddenly yells. "Can you hear me Grandpa? It's Patrick and I miss you grandpa!" He waits.

"Grandpa, it's me, Patrick! Can you hear me?" He rises his head up and looks at his grandmother. A look of confusion is on his young face as he looks at the marker. Then he stands up, looking around, trying desperately to understand. Sadly, he looks back at the grave marker as he begins to comprehend.

"Grandma, I don't think he can hear me," he states dejectedly. "Are you sure he knows we're here?" He continues, "Are you sure grandpa is here?"

"Yes, Patrick, he's here but his spirit is in Heaven," Mary tries to explain. How do you explain death to a child she thinks to herself? She wishes Tom were here to explain for her. Damn him for not explaining to his grandson before he died, she thinks. Now it's up for her to do and she is uncomfortable. She dabs the tears from her eyes as she tries to explain.

"Patrick, Grandpa is in Heaven, remember? He can hear you, but you cannot hear him. You can talk to him but he cannot talk to you. Do you understand?"

The young boy, puzzled, looking up in to the sky, suddenly booms, "Grandpa, I miss playing Lagos with you! I wish you could talk to me!"

Mary replies, "I'm sure he misses playing Lagos with you, too."

"Grandpa, I love you!" Patrick waits, looking again at the grave marker his eyes fill with tears, one cascades down his cheek.

There is a moment of silence, each have their own thoughts. A gentle breeze blows some pink plum petals past them. Hostas have begun to leaf out beneath a large moss covered lava rock. A Robin catches a large, fat worm for her young. Patrick is holding Great grandma's hand now.

"Grandma," Patrick calls softly, tugging gently at great-grandma's arm. Then, louder he shouts, "Grandma!"

"What is it, Patrick?" asks Grandma softly, a tear running down her cheek, a Kleenex in her hand.

"I have to go potty!"

Mary pauses for a moment, looking sadly down at the grave. "I miss you, Thomas Southerland." A moment passes. Finally, looking at Patrick she says softly, "Yes, it's time to go." Hand-in-hand they leave.

Another pink petal is taken by the gentle breeze and placed carefully upon the creeks current. A nest of baby robins crane their necks, mouths open, each knowing their mother will feed them part of the worm she has readied.

From a distance, a crow watches the nest with hungry anticipation, waiting for mom to leave.

And, as Grandma and Patrick's car exits the cemetery, an unshaven, dirty, obese man pauses for a moment with his tree trimmer in hand – watching them leave. For a second his respiring deepens, he pulls at his red tattered shirt, which barely covers his huge stomach. He looks back up at the Willow tree he has been trimming. He sees its balanced shape, and graceful lines, and fullness, and he is satisfied. Slowly, he moves to the next tree.

The Tooth Fairy

Madison is tall for second grader. She stands above most boys in her class and she is thin. She has lot of friends; she is good in her school work. However, she has an ADDHD designation. Her parents care about her success and watch over her carefully. She has a best friend named Kylie. They spend a lot of time together, both in school and out of school. Today, Kylie wants Madison to come over to her house right after school because she has an important secret to tell Madison.

Kylie lives three houses down the block from Madison in a two story white house with green shutters. Her bedroom is upstairs and you can see Madison's house from the bedroom window. Kylie' room has Thomasville furniture that includes a double bed, a large armoire and a small student desk. Often, she and Madison take turns using the desk to complete their homework assignments. Sometimes they are at the desk together if one is having a problem with the homework. Kylie has lost a front tooth.

Kylies' father, Kyle McBrewister, is a successful assistant bank manager whose career is marked for a bank president position in the near future. He is handsome, out-going, and loves fishing and football. He's been known to have his men friends over to watch the Sunday games on the wide screen. He is sure that one day his three years old son, Kevin, will become a great school athlete and go to college.

Kyle's wife, Katie, is an attractive dark haired mother who also works outside the home as a secretary at the local library. She wears startling red-rimmed glasses. All the children in the neighborhood love Kyle and Katie McBrewister. And, the McBrewisters love children.

Madison arrived at the McBrewister house at three-thirty in the afternoon and knocked on the front door. Kylie answered the door but before Madison could enter the house, Kylie stepped quickly out on the porch and took a long look up the street and down the street.

"What is wrong?" asked Madison. She is puzzled by Kylie's behavior. All afternoon at school, Kylie had acted funny and mysterious.

"Nothing, Madison," Kylie answered in a hushed tone. Continuing, she said, "I have a big secret to share with you and you can't share it with anyone." Satisfied that no one else was in the neighborhood; Kylie took Madison by the arm and pushed her into the house. Madison was perplexed and curious all at the same time.

Madison hadn't had time for a snack and was hungry. She asked Kylie if she had something for a snack. Kylie directed her out into the kitchen and said, "Yes, there some milk and cookies we can have. But hurry, mommy and Kevin will be home soon. And, don't make a mess, thank you."

"What did you want to tell me?" Madison asked as she was getting her snack. Kylie looked around as if people might be all around. She said she couldn't tell Madison anything until they were up in her bedroom.

"Did the Tooth Fairy bring you money?" Madison asked, knowing Kylie had planned to put her newly lost front tooth under her pillow last night. "Yes," Kylie replied quickly, looking around again half expecting someone to appear from nowhere. "And, she's not a woman."

"What?" Madison replied looking at Kylie as if she had lost her mind.

"We can't talk about it down here."

She made Madison hurry up with her snack and as they were leaving the kitchen, they heard the back door open. It was Kylie's mother and Kevin. Mother sang out, "We're home, Kylie, as she helped Kevin through the door.

"Hi, Mom," Kylie said hurriedly as she ushered Madison up the stairway. "Madison and I will be in my room."

"Ok, dear. Do your homework!"

Madison looked around Kylie's room to see if she could discover the mystery but as usual, the room was neat as a pin. The bedroom window was open but Kylie went over quickly and closed it. Then she did something Madison had never seen her do before. She pulled the shade down.

"Kylie, what is the big secret?" Madison asked. "Tell me."

"No, wait," She said as she checked the bedroom door to make sure it was closed. "We have to be careful. If this got out to the other kids my dad would be very mad."

"Mad?" Madison questioned. "Mad about what?"

"Well, you know about my dad helping me pull out my front tooth yesterday," Kylie stated, fully serious now, leaning close to Madison.

"Yeah, what of it?" Madison replied impatiently. "It's not that big of deal."

Kylie replied in a hushed tone, "I know, I know but listen to this." Madison sat on the bed ready for the story.

"Like I told you at school my dad helped me pull out my front tooth that was loose. Well, after we got it done he said for me to put it under my pillow and the Tooth Fairy would come and take it. And that **she** would leave some money." Kylie emphasized "she." Then, Kylie waited a moment for all that to sink in with Madison.

Madison just sat there staring at her and said flatly, "Yeah, so?"

"She wasn't a she," Kylie confided. Madison was still puzzled.

"She wasn't a she?" Madison repeated. "I don't get it?"

"Madison, the Tooth Fairy isn't a woman. She's a man," Kylie declared in a secretive tone. "A man, Madison; my Daddy!"

"Your dad?" Madison questioned looking at Kylie.

"Yes, my Daddy." She knew Madison doubted her so she added, "It was my dad putting the money under my pillow. I woke up when he was doing it but I acted like I was sleeping. He doesn't know I know."

Madison sat for a moment, thinking. Then it began to sink in and she became more and more excited. She jumped off the bed, grabbed Kylie, and began yelling how cool this was. Kylie tried to restrain Madison's excitement and calm her down. She told Madison to be quiet and calm down, that she did not want her mother and bother to hear.

"If Daddy knew I knew I am sure he would be upset," Kylie said to Madison. She grabbed Madison by the shoulders and looked Madison straight in her eyes and in her most serious seven-year old voice said, "I'm only telling you because you're my best friend in the whole wide world. You cannot tell anyone; anyone!"

"I won't," said Madison and even more seriously pledged, "I swear it, pins and needles in my eye."

"Good," answered Kylie. "We better get our homework done. Let's not ever talk about this again."

* * * * *

That evening Madison was gloomy, morose, and blue. Her mother noticed, but was giving her time to work out the issue, knowing that in the end she would ask advice. When Madison had trouble with changing schools, last fall she acted like this and then after a couple of days, she asked mom for help. They had talked it through, mom listening to all the problems of changing schools and making new friends and getting adjusted to a new routine. It worked out; hopefully nothing has changed now Mom thought.

"Mom, I have something I need to tell you about," Madison said quietly while getting ready to bush her teeth before going to bed. "I'm worried about Mr. McBrewister."

"Mr. McBrewister?" Madison's Mom questioned. "Is he alright?

"I don't know," Madison replied. "He does a lot of traveling every night visiting all the kids."

"He does?" Mom asked. "What kids does he visit?"

"All the kids who have lost their teeth. Gosh, how does he do that?" She was puzzled and mystified. "Imagine, trying to get all that money distributed. Good thing he works at a bank."

"Money?" Mom just looked at her.

"Yeah, money," she stated with quizzical admiration. "And, all the driving he must do. I don't see how he can get up for work the next morning."

"Driving?" Her Mom said blankly.

"Mom, what do you think he does with all those teeth he collects?" Madison asked, and then quickly added, "Are they any good for anything?"

"Uh," was the only sound mom could make as she tried to not looked perplexed and give an answer that wouldn't be wide of the mark. Finally, Mom said, "Madison slow down and tell me what you are talking about."

Madison just stood there looking at her mother impatiently and said seriously, "Mom, the Tooth Fairy is not a woman." Then she added with authority, "Mr. McBrewister is the Tooth Fairy."

"What!"

"It true mom. Kylie told me today when I was over at her house doing homework. Oh, do you know about math groups?" Madison stated with the honesty only a child of six could have.

"Groups, Uh, math groups?" Mom replied. "No, first let's talk about this Tooth Fairy thing."

"Mom, Kylie told me when she went to bed the other night her dad told her to put her tooth under her pillow and the Tooth Fairy would bring money for the tooth. And, she did." She paused to let her mother think about that.

Her mother, being very serious now, just looked at her.

"Well, she waked up and saw her Dad putting money under her pillow and taking the tooth," Madison explained. "I am so worried about him." She shuddered a bit at the thought of Mr. McBrewister out all night picking up teeth and leaving money. "Good thing he works at a bank," she thought out loud.

A small, tight smile at the very corner of mom's mouth appeared and she turned her head away while trying to determine how to handle this "crisis." She knew this was one of those moments she would share with Madison later in life, one they would both laugh about. Madison was clearly concerned for Mr. McBrewister's health and welfare.

"Wait until Kylie's father hears this one," she thought, giggling to herself.

Then seriously she said to Madison, "Madison, listen to me! I think it's wonderful that you are worried about Mr. McBrewster but believe me he knows what he's doing. So don't worry, he will be fine. Also, I think for now we had better keep Kylie's secret a secret. After all, she's your best friend and you wouldn't want to betray her trust would you?"

Madison thought for a moment, then looked at her mother and said, "You right Mom, thanks." She thought for another moment, then moved on, asking, "What do you know about math groups?"

That night, lying in bed, Madison looked at her mother as she came alongside her to give her a kiss good night. She said, "I love you, Mommy."

Later, as she walked slowly down the stairs, Mom thought about the Tooth Fairy and smiled warmly to herself, "Sweet!"

The Shooter

It falls quietly, the snow, each flake coming straight down, landing like a feather on a breezeless day. At first, the ground shows through the thin layer of flakes but as time passes the flakes become thick and a bank of white forms that is like a mother's bright white sheets on the clothesline. Soft like them, too.

Like people, each snow flake is unique with its own personality, its own individuality, like people in a crowd. Most flakes soon become indistinguishable, and a snow bank forms. Each bank has a shape and a personality of its own, melding all the individual flakes and making itself into a greater personality; a mass multitude.

Yet, there are always a few special flakes that set themselves apart from the crowd, a few more noteworthy than the rest, a few which are loners, that won't conform but somehow become distinguished. And, of those non-conformists, most are extinguished quickly. Nevertheless, in that moment, they catch our attention before they are taken. Frankie Madero was such an individual.

The grounds of the hospital are covered with snow, making it difficult for the ambulances to reach the emergency entrance. Carefully, they maneuver up a steep slope and park under the ambulance entrance portico. The front of the ambulance is exposed, but its rear exit doors are protected by a sizable covered entrance. The driver jumps out his door and hurries his way to the rear to help take the victim out of the ambulance and roll him into ER. The paramedic yells for the driver to go ahead into the ER and find a trauma nurse immediately.

The paramedic remains with the victim, metrically squeezing the airbag to force air into the victim's lungs causing inhalation through artificial means. The paramedic knows the victim is clinically dead, but procedure still calls for his best effort. "Hospice be damned," he thinks as he and his other EMT wheel the victim in to ER along with a nurse who is now operating the airbag.

"Room three," yells the Charge Nurse to the cluster of people as they sweep the victim through the entrance doors.

Two other nurses now join the precession, walking besides the victim as they all rapidly move him into Room Three, which is closest to the entry doors.

The paramedic notes that two police cars have quietly driven up - one parks behind the ambulance, the other boxing in the front. The officers have gotten out of their cars and are following as the victim is wheeled into room three.

"Vitals?" the Charge Nurse asks as the victim is transferred from the gurney to the hospital bed.

The Paramedic begins calling out vital signs and what has happened to the victim, both at the scene and during the ride to the hospital. He expresses no opinion as to the living status of the victim and concludes his narration with "Male, 19, gunshot wound to base of the skull!"

A doctor has entered the room and is examining the victim. He calls for a blood pressure reading and vital signs. It is here the victim becomes the patient and the team will use all their skills to save the patient's life. "Take the patient's vitals," he calls out. He is told all are flat, with his stethoscope he listens intently for a heartbeat. A nurse is checking the patient's ankle; another, the wrist; another, the neck - each looking for a sign of life. "No pulse!" one yells!

"Let's get the Crash Team in here, Stat!" the doctor yells.

The "Code 99" goes out seconds later over the hospital intercom. Nurses and technicians from all departments of the hospital begin the protocol response that will hopefully save the patient from death. Within minutes, twenty people, each with a special job, are milling around the door as the doctor calls out specific procedures that are known to resuscitate a patient, even if only for a limited time.

It is a Dance of Life that the Crash Team performs, like a fine ballet, each dancer knows just when and how to respond, each dancer coming forward as their specialty is called for. Each dances their part in perfect unison with their teammates: precise, delicate, a beauty one can imagine as a team of ballerinas moving across a stage to a mesmerizing symphony.

Suddenly, a shout rings out! "I have a weak pulse," announces the nurse at the patient's ankle. Another order comes from the doctor. The cast is once again in motion; a ventilator tube is now protruding from the mouth of the patient. The doctor calls for an injection. A ballerina gracefully, deftly takes a syringe handed-off from a dancer in the back, support row. The injection is momentarily made into the IV site; the nurse now returns the syringe back to the secondary row.

"Ventilate," shouts the doctor! A machine begins to hum, lights begin to flash and an alarm sounds. The patient's chest rises slightly, then relaxes as the air pumps in and out, the rhythmic sounds of life being forced into the patient's body, never is a beat missed nor a breath of air forgotten. This machine will work tirelessly hour after hour, day after day, week after week. It will give the patient his best chance to mend and to heal. To the family, it will give them time to adjust, to contemplate and to comprehend how their loved one got to this point in his life. Also, it will give them a tenuous gift: Hope.

The nurse at patient's ankles listens intently and then quietly announces, "Pulse, flat!" Outside, the snow continues to fall quietly, building a bank of snow even higher, one less defined, imprecise, fuzzy; as a life in limbo.

The patient's family has arrived, milling around the emergency waiting room. Thirty Hispanics not quite knowing what to do; each talking to one another; each trying to find out what happened, and each trying to comprehend.

The family matriarch is sitting regally, holding a rosary, waiting to be told how her son is doing. How strong he is. How he is beating death. How he is going to recover. Already, twice, she has said a rosary to Our Lady of Guadalupe. Our Lady has never failed her.

The matriarch has sent her second son for the priest, Father Mezcal. Her husband sits by himself, in his own world. As usual, he is of no help to her. An elder daughter comes back from the emergency room to tell la jefe that her son, Francisco Madero, has been moved to the Critical Care unit. That the immediate family can visit in one hour.

Frankie's mother sits for a moment, pondering her next move. Standing up, she states flatly, "No, we go now!" Then she hesitates, she doesn't know where Critical Care is located.

"Donde," she asks her daughter hurriedly. "Where, where!"

The Critical Care unit is on the second floor behind closed doors, opened only by entering a code on a key pad, or by the Charge Nurse using a switch at her desk from inside the unit. To talk with the Charge Nurse, a visitor has to push a button on a speaker phone mounted on the wall outside the entry doors. A sign written only in English explains the required procedure.

Frankie's mother has had her daughter interpret the sign and make the call to allow them access to her beloved oldest son. She enters a world she has never seen before. She is frightened, but determined to find her son. She knows her Frankie; she knows he's a fighter.

"My Frankie, where he is?" she asks in English. A nurse points to his room.

The Intensive Critical Care Unit at Memorial is a long hallway affair with ten rooms on one side of the hallway and nurse stations along the other side. The hallway is dimly lit, but each room has a large helix-light above the bed. The mood of the unit is intense, professional and sustaining. The nurses are the best of the best, each having passed strict criteria to be part of this elite team. Each room is equipped with a mechanical ventilator to assist breathing using an endotracheal tube; plus, cardiac monitors with telemetry directly hooked to a nurse's station; a defibrillator to shock the heart back into rhythm; and, dialysis equipment in the event of renal failure. There are computer screens and monitors mounted everywhere in the room and at all of the nursing stations. Every patient is scrutinized every second, twenty-four hours a day, seven-days a week. Nothing is left to chance. Every breath is heard. Every movement of the patient is documented. Each nurse records their every course of action in detail, which doctors read and re-read, and re-read, again and again. All this hardware and personnel exists for just one singular purpose—to give the patient a chance at life.

When visitors or family members walk in for the first time, it is almost too overwhelming. One can see their stress, even feel it. Not only is their loved one in trouble and sick or hurt, but there is all this equipment and all these tubes: the endotracheal tube; a catheter protruding from below the covers; a nasogastric tube extending from the patient's abdomen; and, the ominous intravenous tower with its continuous drip, drip, drip. For a mother, its heart wrenching and anguishing to see her first-born in this condition, all of those tubes and all of those machines.

Mama looks at her son laying there with this mass of tubes and machines surrounding his bed. His chest moves slowly up and down as she hears the ventilator pump forcing air into his lungs and then relaxing. At his bedside, she slowly reaches out and gently places a hand on his arm.

Softly she says, "Frankie. Frankie, *es mama.*"

But there's no response as Frankie's chest moves up and down to the rhythm of the machine. Mama stands looking at him. The endotracheal tube juts from his mouth like a snake trying to free itself. Tears fill her large eyes and roll slowly down her cheeks. Her oldest son is in trouble, and she doesn't know what to do or how to get these people to help more. She stands there uneasy, touching his arm again, and again, and looking at all the lights and hearing all the sounds. The sight most promising and one she comprehends is the heaving of Frankie's chest. He must still be fighting, and she knows he will win. She looks expectantly at nurses entering the room. "Gracias a Dios," she says to herself.

Two female nurses enter Frankie's room and begin checking the monitor. One is asking the other about his heart rate and why is it so fast? The older nurse replies, "It's because of the medicine given. It purposely increases the heart rate to move the blood through the body and aureate the cells." She leans close to her trainee and whispers, "Actually, Bonnie, the patient is clinically dead. We're keeping him on life support to help the family and the police. He came in dead on arrival, but because it involves a police shooting, we have been told to use all heroics possible. As soon as the police and family say OK, we'll pull the plug."

As the nurses do their work and talk, Frankie's mother is remembering when her first son was born. A first-born son in the Hispanic culture is special. She remembers his wet head and body as it slid out the birth canal and into the hands of the waiting mid-wife. They used the family knife, which had come down through the generations of her family, to cut the cord. The cut was swift and the knot was expertly tied, the mid-wife having done hundreds of these birthing's in the village of Las Otates. The village of her family lay just south of Nogales, where they had farmed for countless generations. When news came from the North about jobs and "big money" to be made, she knew that her family must go to America del Norte.

The mid-wife placed little Frankie in her arms, who was tightly bound in a blanket and crying. "Un Niño sano," declared the mid-wife. The mid-wife was beaming as she looked at the healthy baby boy she had just delivered. Then she turned and left the room to announce the birth to the rest of the family, and to the proud father.

Frankie's young father came into the room to see his newborn son. He stood looking at his wife and his son; his first child was a son. God had blessed his family and he made a quick sign of the cross before kissing his wife on her forehead. "Gracias, mi amore," he said. "For my son, I thank you."

Today, he stood at the foot of the hospital bed looking at his son not knowing what to do or what to think. He'd heard the policea had shot him. Had shot his son? What is the matter with these gringos? Always they are after my son. He's a good boy. He looks at his wife and asks, "Que esta?"

The two police officers sit at a nursing desk directly across from Frankie's room, talking softly with each other. One answers the cellular that rings every few moments. He listens intently, and then hangs up.

"Who is this guy?" The one officer asked the other in a hushed whisper?

"Francisco Madero," replied the second officer, a lieutenant. Reading the police report to his colleague, he continued, "Wanted as a suspect in a gang shooting that took place two months ago over on Sixth Street. I guess Casey and Mary ran across him over on Eighteenth Street and tried to arrest him, but he resisted."

Right then the cell phone rang again. The lieutenant picks up the phone and opens the case report. Putting the phone to his ear, he said professionally, "Lt. Andrew." Andrew was a big man, almost 6'6", broad across the shoulders, handsome and articulate, he listened a moment and then said, "Understood, Captain." He closed his cell phone and turned to his partner.

"Captain wants us not to say anything to the family about taking this guy off the ventilator. Apparently, there is some question about police brutality in the Hispanic community." He motioned to the nurse and began explaining the situation to her.

In Frankie's room, a nurse is pretentiously checking the monitors and writing down the numbers on to a chart as Frankie's mother watches. Mama remembered the first time she brought Frankie here, how high his fever had been, his crying, and how he was sensitive to touch. They'd told her that it was meningitis, and he need to be in the hospital for a few days. She remembered her fear then, and the long walk up to the children's intensive care unit.

Her first-born son had been sick. The entire family was there supporting them. The crowd was large outside the intensive children care unit. She knew then, as she knows now, with God's help, Frankie will beat it and get well. He's my first son, my first-born – he has to make it. He such a good boy, my boy; my first-born.

Oh, how could this happen? La policia are bad people, she thinks as she gazes out at the two officers. Look at them laughing and being happy while my son fights for his life. What is wrong with these cerdos, those pigs? She almost spits on the ground before remembering where she is. They almost killed Frankie, but they didn't. He will make it. She looks at her husband. "The useless one", she thinks to herself.

He stands by the side of the bed watching his son's chest move slowly up and down. His tan, baggy pants, and flannel shirt hide his years out in the fields picking and doing farm work. These gringos he smirks, thinking to himself, "They've killed my oldest, my son who has helped provide for the family since he was eight years old. He would bring me a cartoon of cigarettes once a week from the convenience store down on the corner. Such a good boy; never asked for money. When he was twelve and the car broke-down who was it that got the money to repair it? Frankie, my oldest son, he was a good worker. My son and his friends went out and did some work for the man at the old house, and he paid them. He paid them good! That was the same house the police raided a few months later. He said it was unfair to the man living there. Frankie had to find someone else to do work for. He was good boy, never out of work, and always he brought home money for his Mama and me. Now they've killed my son. I know he's dead, look at the machines. Que es todos, what is all this?"

Outside of the intensive care unit's double doors is the waiting area for family and friends. Normally, it's immediate family members; maybe a friend is there, everyone one is waiting for some news. The friends normally come and stay for a while, then leave, saying they'll be back or saying to call when some news comes. "Call when something changes," they say. They leave, almost always feeling a little guilty, yet, a little relieved.

Today, the family and friends of Francisco Madero number fifty-five, including a few children who are running around. Insensitive white people sometimes think these children are terrible, that their parents don't know how to discipline. Yet, the Hispanic parents are showing no signs of their children's behavior as a bother to them or anyone else.

They are all there to support Frankie and his parents, neither of whom has come out of the ICU doors.

Father Mezcal is talking with Frankie's younger brother and his sisters. "God is with Frankie," he is saying while making a sign of the cross, which he does often. "You must pray for his soul and for God's grace. That God may bless Frankie and bring him back to us."

He looks earnestly over the crowd, "Pray my people, pray for Frankie's recovery. Pray for his soul that if he should die that he will go with God." He makes a sweeping sign of the cross over the crowd. Others in the large group are making signs of the cross or are looking for their rosaries, which the women carry in their purses. A child sends a lamp crashing to the floor, broken glass scatters over the floor, stopping at the feet of the Padre. He looks earnestly at the child then makes the sign of the cross.

At the other end of the waiting area, a police captain walks to the employee's entrance of the ICU, looks over the crowd, wondering how they are going to tell this group the bad news. He hesitates for a moment, before disappearing through the unit's the doors.

"Andrew," the Captain calls out to the lieutenant at the desk. "Bring me up to speed. What's been going on here?"

"Well, Captain," Lt. Andrew replies while pointing at Frankie's room, "That's the mother and father in there. The rest of the family is out in the waiting area. Large group, I hear. Haven't been out to look, yet."

A nod by the Captain affirms this point.

The lieutenant continues, "They've been visiting the subject's room in ones and twos. For the most part, they've been quiet and cooperative. A priest came in and administered Last Rites. Internal security has been keeping an eye on them, then reporting to us. As you probably know, the patient is basically brain dead but the family hasn't been told that. The priest left and I think he's in the outer area leading prayers with the family and friends."

"Yeah, it's Father Mezcal," the Captain replied. "He's alright. I think he can keep them in-line." He paused for a moment, thinking, and then continued, "I'm worried as to what will happen when we finally announce he's dead."

"Captain," Lt. Andrew suggests, "we better had wait for a few hours. Let's let them sit awhile. The crowd should thin out towards the middle of the night."

"Yeah, good idea," Captain George said as he stops a nurse to inquire who the Duty Nurse is.

"I am," She smiles. "My name is Agnes Stouffer. What's up?"

"How long can we delay announcing the patient in 242's death?" the Captain asks.

"As long as you want," she replied. "He is on a ventilator and it will pump until we pull the plug. We've just been waiting on you guys and the family to accept what has happened."

Captain George paused for a moment, looking around the unit, his eyes stop at the patient's room. He is looking at the mother standing next to her son's bed. He could see her torment, her deep fear, and her questioning as to what will happen next with her son. He knows the Hispanic culture, he knows the pain, and he knows how the barrio will gather around and support the family no matter what.

"We need to wait until the middle of the night before pulling the plug," he says to the nurse and his lieutenant. "Let's do it in the middle of the night after the crowd has thinned out and most people have gone to bed."

Then he adds, "Have security encourage the families to take the children home about nine o'clock." He knows that Hispanic families will understand that.

"Can I ask what this guy did?" asked the nurse.

"Yeah, let me brief both you and my officers," George replies taking a notebook out of his shirt pocket. He flips a few pages and then begins, "Francisco I. Madero is a known "shooter" for one of the local gangs. Two months ago, he was commissioned to kill a local, rival drug dealer. Instead of shooting just the dealer, this guy shoots the dealer and his entire family. He killed the dealer and his five-year-old daughter at the front door of their home. He then entered the house and shot the wife who was hovering over their youngest daughter, a three year old." He paused a moment, then continued, "The bullet from that shot went through the mother and lodged into the three year old's arm. The mother got up and somehow ran out of the house and got away. We think the arrival of one of our units alerted the shooter and he took off." The captain stopped for moment to allow his audience to digest the information. "Not a nice guy, huh?"

"A jewel," Lt. Andrew answered with bitter harshness in his voice.

The Captain continued with the narrative, "This morning one of our units spotted him and attempted to arrest him, then got into a struggle. During the struggle, this guy pulls out a gun. The assisting officer pulled her weapon and fired into his skull. The shot hit him at the back and base of his skull."

The Captain paused for a moment, reviewed his notes and continued. "Anyway, we need to wait until the middle of the night to pull the plug on this guy," the Captain explained. "Get hospital security to encourage the family and friends to go home later this evening."

Frankie's mother is standing at the foot of his bed. The unit is quiet and the evening sun is setting low. It's that time between the activity of the day and coziness of the night, when there is a calm that settles across the earth while people get ready for an evening with family, or with friends, or just to watch the news. But this night this Mom stands there looking at her oldest son, remembering. Tears fill her eyes as she reaches out to lay her hand on his foot that is exposed from under the covers. She cries out, "Frankie, te quiero asi, I love you so. Why this?"

Lt. Andrew looks up from his desk. He remembers to call his wife to tell her he will be late. Picking up the phone, he dials.

Outside, in the twilight between the day and the night, snow continues to fall in large flakes that settle lightly on a bank. Tomorrow night's evening news will give all the headlines, the sports, and the economic report. Then there will be a short sound bite about a nineteen-year-old Hispanic man dying, who was the main suspect in the execution-style slaying of a man and his five-year-old daughter. By then, the bank of snow outside the hospital will have started to melt into the earth and people will shake their heads in disbelief. And, a mother's heart will mourn her first-born son.

Ray's Malt Shop

It sat at the corner of Wilcox Street and Randolph. It was not large by 1949 standards, nor was it particularly attractive, but it was busy most of the time. Mostly with locals who lived within a few blocks of the shop. Ray owned it. Everyone agreed he cooked the best burgers in town and made the tastiest malts.

Ray's Malt Shop was one of the earliest malt shops to have walk-up service. One didn't need to enter the neatly-kept shop to place an order; one could walk up to one of the two windows that opened onto the sidewalk. Beginning at 11:30 a.m. a line would form at the windows and as people placed their orders, the sidewalk became the waiting area.

Ray would be at the grill, which was to one side of the service windows, and as the orders were placed he would flip a raw burger patty, or hot dog, onto the grill. By noon, the grill would be crammed full of patties and hot dogs; the sidewalk crowded with customers laughing and talking. As the meat cooked, Ray would prepare the buns. He had big bowls of iceberg lettuce sitting in ice with brimming stacks of fresh leafs. Next to the lettuce were bowls of red, beef-steak tomatoes, all neatly cut and ready to be thrown onto the buns. Right of the tomatoes was stacks of uniformly sliced onions. And, lastly, at the head of his condiment table Ray had jars of mayonnaise, dill and sweet pickles, bottles of catsup, and bowls of mustard. There was even fresh relish, handmade by Ray, for the hot dogs.

The girl at the window would take an order from a customer, writing it down in restaurant shorthand then yelling the order to Ray who already had heard order and had flipped the right amount of meat onto the grill.

"One with - hold the goop - mayo only - add cheese - and burn the bun," the girl would holler-out!

The grilling pirouette would begin. Ray would throw the meat onto the grill, quickly twirl down and retrieved a slice of cheese from the under-the-counter refrigerator as he spiraled up and grabbed a plate with his free hand. He gracefully slid the slice of cheese onto the plate, where it waited for the right moment to be positioned on the cooking meat patty. Finally, in a final whirl, he would reach into a plastic bag full of hamburger buns, smartly grab one, open it and place in the commercial toaster that rotated the buns past red-hot elements. His movements were elegant, sophisticated, and stylish.

Watching Ray and his crew work was like watching a beautiful ballet, one in which the dancers moved as a team. Each member knew their role and was accomplished, mostly from the redundancy of having worked there for so long. Few people ever quit on Ray — he was a good boss.

What makes some businesses a success while others of the same nature are gone within a couple of years? It's not an odd question to ask, but it's a question every student of business asks, ponders and comes up with an assortment of reasons. Most make sense; many collapse. The fact is a successful business has many of the same elements and assets of those that fail.

Ray's Malt Shop had several fatal flaws when Ray started the business. The location was terrible. The business was not located on a major thoroughfare. Ray would have done better to look for a location on Gage Avenue where each day more than ten thousand cars passed the intersection of Gage and Wilcox. Instead, Ray chose to place his new venture at the corner of Wilcox and Randolph, where the daily traffic count was less than 500 cars per day.

Another fatal flaw with the shop was the ratio of the customer seating area to the square footage of the kitchen space. When you entered Ray's, there was a counter to your immediate right, which curved around the kitchen, enclosing it from the tables. People who came to sit at one of the five tables had to go up to the counter to order their food. Customers could elect to sit at the oversized counter, a counter Ray built himself, which he unconsciously made really deep. Customers had to stand up on the chrome footrest beneath their stool to reach the salt, pepper, or catsup.

Ray's tables, like his counter, were expansive. Customers, who were lucky enough to find a vacant table, would sit across from one another. They almost had to shout to hear each other. With a high ceiling and plain white walls, noon at Ray's was filled with discordant sounds of people eating, talking, laughing, and bitching. Above the dissonant din came the shouts, "Two cheese, one with, one without, no mayo, ketchup only, dill pickles, hold the tomatoes on the side!" And, there was no table service.

Customers complained about no table service after reading the "No Table Service" sign hanging on the wall. They felt even more offended and slighted when Ray's yelled out their order was ready. "Two cheeseburger, one with, one mayo and pickles only," he would call to no one in particular. Customers would often grumble and curse as they made their way to the counter. Some even had to make two and three trips, bitching all the way.

"Jesus, Ray, can't you hire a waitress, for Christ's sake," one irate customer bellowed as he grabbed his order?

"Can't afford it, Keith!" Ray answered forcefully. Keith muttered something under his breath to which Ray said, "Goddam it, Keith, let me put your lunch in a sack. I'll throw it out the window to you so you can take it back to your shop and eat. Would that be better?"

"Can't do that," Keith shot back, then added as he watched Ray feed hamburger buns into the toaster, "Got the wife for lunch today, Ray. She isn't wanting to get her dress dirty."

Keith's wife sat quietly at one of the big tables saying nothing, but was thinking, "Keith's right." She was due back at her teller window in thirty minutes and didn't want to chance a dirty office. Besides, she had something very special to tell her husband.

Keith Patterson owned the auto repair shop across Randolph Street. Randolph was divided in two by railroad tracks, which made the walk back to his shop slower and more hazardous than normal. This particular day, his wife of two years, Mary Ann, had unexpectedly dropped in for lunch. Happily, Keith told his two employees they were on their own for lunch today. Keith didn't realize Mary Ann had something special to tell him — something very special.

If Keith was Ray's most vocal customer, retired, white-haired Mr. Truman was Ray's quietest; a most courteous patron, a member of a retreating generation. He sat serenely at the same table every day, in the corner, usually by himself; occasionally with his wife. Like most retired men of his age, he had mellowed. Mr. Truman enjoyed Ray's cheeseburgers; people watching, also. Occasionally, he could spot out a patron who was a former student. He'd taught history at the local high school after returning from abroad and graduating Stanford.

At eleven o'clock every weekday, Mr. Truman would start his journey down Palm Avenue. At Randolph, he turned left after checking for cars coming from different directions. Carefully he placed his cane onto the pavement and deliberately crossed the street to the western side of Palm.

When he was half a block from the malt shop, Ray would spot him shuffling slowly down the walk. A shadow of a smile would reflect across Ray's lips as he bent down to retrieve a burger patty; the start of Mr. Truman's cheeseburger.

"One cheese on," Ray would call out. "Pickles and mayo only, start Mr. Truman's fries, well done." Patti, Ray's assistant for the lunch rush would drop a serving of raw potatoes into the fryer. "Truman's down, one cherry coke coming up," Patti would bellow back.

Only minutes passed before the wooden screen door slowly opened and archaic Mr. Truman, formally dressed, would walk-in, taking his place at "his" corner table. The table was usually empty because he ate early. Once asked why he came in so early, he answered that he didn't need to take up the table of a working man.

After sitting down, Mr. Truman took his wallet from inside his suit coat and removed two, one dollar bills and placed them carefully on the table. Returning his wallet to his coat pocket, he then reached into his pants pocket and retrieved a coin purse. Slowly and carefully he would slide the zipper open, extract one quarter and place it with the dollar bills. He always had the exact amount needed to pay for his lunch--$2.25.

Mr. Truman was the one exception to Ray's "No Table Service" sign. When the order was complete, Ray would call out, "Order up!" Patti would grab the cherry Coke (not too much ice), snatch the new plastic basket filled with a cheeseburger and fries, then rush off to Mr. Truman's table. Setting the food down in front of the elderly man, knowingly she flashed him a quick, practiced, maternal smile.

"And, here you are, young lady," Mr. Truman replied, handing her a shiny Mercury-head dime.

Patti looked at the shiny, new dime Mr. Truman had dropped into her hand. With a raised eyebrow, she said sarcastically, "Wow, thank you!" Placing the dime in the pocket of her apron pocket, she raced off to get the next customer waiting to order at the window. He wondered if she realized . . .

Her next customer was young Tommy, who lived across the street from Mr. Truman. Tommy had run down from his house with his best friend, his dog Lady. He had a quarter from his mom. He was intent on a vanilla cone for him and Lady to share. This had been their pattern for most of the summer.

Getting the double scoop cone, young Tommy, along with Lady, would sink down below the service window to eat it. It never occurred to him, as with most six year olds, he and his dog might be in the way of other customers. Lady sat as close to him as possible, careful not to touch the arm holding the ice cream. Her big brown eyes belied her eagerness for a taste of the ice cream, but like all good dogs, she was patient.

Tommy had two or three quick licks, before he offered Lady a lick. The ice cream was already melting in the summer heat. Lady would eagerly, but neatly take her lick. The cool, creamy ice cream felt good on her tongue. One could tell she loved it. Her little brown Spaniel body would tremble with joy as she stood up, then quickly sat down again. She squirmed with anticipation, waiting for the next offer.

After Lady's lick, Tommy would take a lick. Lick, lick, lick, back and forth they went. Greedily they quickly licked the ice cream into oblivion because of the heat. Lady's hot breath probably didn't help either as she panted on the cone. Back and forth went the licking, until suddenly only the cone was left, still filled with creamy ice cream, which Tommy devoured down to the last inch or two, then he offered Lady the tidbit, who gratefully devoured it in one gulp. Both were replete.

"Wasn't that good, girl?" Tommy celebrated. Lady stood up on all fours, happily wagged her stubby tail, looking at her master with all the admiration she could muster. "Yes, that was good; is there more?" she seemingly begged.

"We better head for home, girl," Lady's young master stated. "Mom will wonder where we are. Let's go, girl." As he stood up to leave, Mr. Truman slowly opened the screen door. He, too, was headed for home.

"Hi, Mr. Truman," Tommy greeted Mr. Truman. "Can I help you with the door, Sir?"

"Why thank you, young man," Mr. Truman replied cheerfully. Using his cane, he carefully stepped down and out the door way as young Tommy held the screen door diligently, the way Mom had taught him to do for older people. Lady was circling excitedly around their feet, expeditiously being careful not to get stepped-on or hit by the cane, but wanting to be part of the happenings.

"Mr. Truman," Tommy asked respectfully, "Can we walk home with you?"

"We?" Mr. Truman was craning his neck, looking around to see who Tommy meant by "we." "Oh, you and your little friend," he answered, pointing his cane at Lady. She gave a muffled growl at the cane end then went back to circling around their feet.

"That's Lady, my dog. Lady, be good," Tommy replied. "We shared an ice cream together." As they walked along the sidewalk, Tommy repeatedly called out, "Lady, come." The little reddish-brown dog, tail wagging, tongue hanging out, fell dutifully in step with her young master, if only for a moment.

They walked up the street, away from the malt shop, towards their home street of Palm Avenue. Tommy was remembering everything mom had taught him about respecting older people. Help them when you can, she had said. Suddenly, Tommy realized they weren't talking. What to talk about, he questioned himself? Suddenly, he realized Mr. Truman was asking him a question.

"So, Tommy, it is Tommy isn't it?" Mr. Truman was asking. "What kind of dog do you have there?"

Tommy was stopped by the question. He had never thought to ask. He had never thought to ask his mom. He never thought to ask his dad, either. Dad had just brought her home one day from work and announced that Lady would be his dog. Tommy never thought about what kind of dog she was. "Gosh, Mr. Truman, I don't know," young Tommy answered with honesty.

Mr. Truman took a couple more steps before asking, "Why don't you know?"

"Lady, come here," Tommy called out as Lady wondered out towards the curb. "You stay away from the street, girl." He stepped towards the curb and patted the top of his thigh a couple of times, "Over here, girl. Come on."

"Gosh, Mr. Truman, guess I never asked," Tommy finally replied. Why would Mr. Truman ask me that, Tommy thought? Seemed like a silly question to the young boy as he and Mr. Truman walked slowly home. Tommy didn't notice his senior walking partner appraising him out the corner of his eye.

Mr. Truman then asked, "Don't you think it's important to know?"

"Why?" the boy absently replied. He was still trying to coax his dog from the curb.

Truman came to a stop and placed both his bony hands on his cane and looked down over his glasses at Tommy. "Tommy, do you love Lady?"

"Yes …, of course," Tommy replied hesitantly. Of course, he loved his dog. My dad gave me Lady, of course I love her. Why is Mr. Truman asking me these things he again thought to himself?

"If you love Lady," Mr. Truman asked, "shouldn't you know some basic things about her?"

"I guess so," replied Tommy, uncertain as to what Mr. Truman was asking. He knelt down and gave his dog a big hug, again he told her to stay away from the street. Tommy knew he loved going with Lady to share an ice cream cone. He knew he loved using the baseball to play fetch with her. He knew when he went to bed, he loved having her jump up on the bed and snuggle against him after mom closed the bedroom door. In the morning, at seven-thirty exactly, every morning she would lick his face.

Finally, he decided to ask Dad, then, he said to Mr. Truman, "I'll ask Dad tonight."

"I just wish she'd stay away from street, Mr. Truman," Tommy worried and in a tone almost pleading, he added, "Gosh, I wish she'd stay next to me."

"Keep after her, she'll learn," Mr. Truman replied. "Learn all you can about her, then, come tell me."

"Why, Mr. Truman?" Tommy asked.

Mr. Truman's eyes sparkled as he answered, "Because I'm curious, and you need to know more about her."

"Why?" Tommy questioned.

Mr. Truman reflexed a moment as he limped slowly down the sidewalk, then said, "Because when you love someone, or something, you need to know everything about them. It will make your little friend feel secure. If she can feel your love, then she'll listen to you. Plus, you'll take better care of her."

They continued to walk slowly down the street when out of the blue Tommy exclaimed, "Lady and I play war together, Mr. Truman. She's my rescue dog. When I get shot by the Japs, she comes and rescues me."

"Really," was all Mr. Truman could muster, "Really!"

Without thinking, Tommy asked innocently, "Mr. Truman, why do you limp? And have a cane? Were you in the war, or somethin'?"

As Tommy waited for his answer, they came to the corner of Randolph and Palm. Mr. Truman lived directly across the street from young Tommy. Both houses were in the middle of the block. He paused a moment, trying to decide if he should cross Palm to his side of the street, or continue to walk with Lady and Tommy.

Mr. Truman looked up and down Randolph, then down Palm to his house. He started to cross the street but suddenly turned down the same walk with Tommy and his dog.

"Yes, I was in war," he quietly answered the young man's question. "The Great War!"

A flurry of excitement whipped through Tommy. He hurriedly told how his Dad wasn't able to go to war. How he went each Saturday to the Alcazar Theater to watch war movies. He said he really didn't like to go to the movies on Saturday because he couldn't take Lady. "I do like the war movies," He stated but added, he didn't like leaving Lady home alone. But it was OK because his Mom was there. She loves Lady, too. "But, she makes Lady stay out in the backyard by herself," Tommy moaned. "I wish she'd let her in the house." He thought a moment, then, asked, "Were you in the Pacific? Did you fight the Japs? What was it like? Lady, get out of the street!"

"Tommy, I wasn't in World War II," Mr. Truman quietly answered. The memories of a long ago war swept over Mr. Truman causing him to shiver and withdraw into himself.

Then, suddenly, he realized Tommy was asking another question — oh, these six-year olds.

"If you didn't fight the Japs," Tommy questioned, "Who'd you fight?"

Mr. Truman looked down at Tommy, then, his gaze settled on a car speeding down the street towards them. "Better get control of Lady," Mr. Truman called out to Tommy.

"Lady, here girl," Tommy said quickly. The young boy ran quickly to the curb as the car approached, "Lady, get out of the street!" The car narrowly missed Lady as the young dog dodged the car, then raced to her master.

Tommy bent over and patted Lady on the head, "Lady, you got'ta stay out of the street. The cars can't see ya, girl."

"Mr. Truman, what am I going to do with her?" Tommy impatiently asked the old man.

Mr. Truman replied with a question, "Do you have a leash for her? Maybe a leash would help until you get her trained." He, too, had been nervous about her running into the street, thankful the traffic was light on their street. This last car came a little too close for comfort; extremely fast, too.

"Gosh, Mr. Truman, we've been going to the malt shop all summer," Tommy replied, then finished with "I never thought of a leash."

"Maybe you should, young man," Truman replied.

"OK," Tommy replied. A moment passed then he remembered, "Mr. Truman, did you fight the Japs?"

"The Japs?" Mr. Truman reflected. "Gosh, No! I was in th…"

Without thinking, the young boy interrupted the old gentleman with, "You didn't fight the Japs?" Tommy looked at Mr. Truman questioningly, not fully understanding the older man's age. "I thought everybody fought the Japs—like in the movies."

As the old man, young boy, and Lady moved towards the middle of the block, Mr. Truman's natural even-tempered good nature was taking a slight hit. He looked down at the young boy who was now more interested in his dog than in Mr. Truman's answer.

"Lady, get out of the street," Tommy cried. "Com' on girl, over here." Then, he looked up at Mr. Truman and spit out, "What?"

"Lady ran out in the street," young Tommy cried out. Tommy grabbed Lady by her collar, then, placed both hands on her ears making her look straight into his eyes. Nose to nose with his little dog, Tommy said forcefully, "Lady, you got'ta stay out of the street."

Lady looked at Tommy, seemly a moment of understanding passed between them, when, suddenly, her tongue slipped out quickly and licked away a spot of dried ice cream on Tommy' chin. Tommy jumped back a little, grabbing his chin and looking exasperated.

"Mr. Truman, she won't listen," Tommy exclaimed. He looked at Mr. Truman expectantly; Mr. Truman would have an idea of what to do.

"Actually, I don't know what to say, Tommy," Mr. Truman replied. He thought a moment, crumpled his brows, adding, "I think you better try the leash."

Tommy was bent over, holding Lady by the collar. When he looked up, he saw he was in front of his house. Letting go of Lady's collar, she made a mad dash for the front of the house. Stopping short of the porch, she turned back towards Tommy and Mr. Truman wagging her tail madly, her tongue dancing out the side of her jowls. Her innocence, her zeal, and her obvious affection melted into Tommy's core.

Mr. Truman was waving goodbye to Tommy as he turned to cross the street to his house.

Tommy was waving wildly back as he ran to Lady, then, yelled, "Good-bye, Mr. Truman. Sorry you didn't get to fight the Japs."

"We'll talk about it later, Tommy," as he carefully placed his cane on to the pavement, thinking to himself that Tommy would get to read a book someday in the future about The Great War.

With that, the old veteran entered his modest home and went directly to his small office library. In his office, on one wall, was a "Teacher of The Year" certificate. The other three walls were lined with books, hundreds of books.

From one of the shelves, he took down a pine wood box. Quietly he sat down at his desk and opened the lid. The box interior was lined with green velvet. Pinned neatly to the velvet were three military metals — two Purple Hearts, and in the center, larger than the hearts was a metal cross with two crossed swords. The ribbon was a military green with orange stripes.

Mr. Truman reached his fingers into the box, lightly rubbing his fingertips over the La Croix de Guerre. It was awarded to him in 1916. Tears swelled to eyes, memories coursed. With a heavy hand, he closed the box, replacing it meticulously back on the shelf in its spot.

One nice thing about books, he thought, they will be there when you're ready for them. "That's how it is with books," he said out loud quietly, "They'll wait for you, young man."

* * * * * *

Summers swelter, in this part of the country, especially in late August and early September when public schools reconvene after a summer hiatus. The heat is dry and hot.

There is no wind to blow across one's skin and reduce the searing of the sun's rays. Perspiration runs ramped, draining bodies of potassium; people become depleted with exhaustion, doctors gave out salt tablets like candy to a waiting public demanding relief.

But, there was a new weapon against this repressive heat, the air conditioner, water cooled with a fan blowing air over moistened organic coils. The fact that the fan blew air at a high rate of speed was itself a respite from the heat. Unfortunately, the malt shop didn't have one of these "new-fangled contraptions" as Ray like to put it.

Keith Patterson, Keith the mechanic, whose shop was across from Ray's malt shop had one. It was mounted up on the roof and blew cool air through a vent in the ceiling. Keith and his three mechanic employees thought it was terrific. "Cools the shop way down," Keith like to brag. Of course, when they opened the big garage doors to move cars in and out of the work area, all the cool air was lost.

"When you getting air-conditioning, Ray?" Keith would chide Ray. He took great joy in mocking Ray in front of customers. "You need to get air-conditioning, Ray," he would call out to Ray in front of the busy lunch crowd. Many of the customers would nod their heads in agreement. Yes, yes, you do Ray.

"Damn it, Keith," Ray would blurt back. "I don't need air-conditioning for two weeks out of the year." Keith would laugh as many of the customers would groan and wish for air-conditioning. "Yes, you do, Ray," Keith would laughingly hammer back at Ray.

"No, I don't Keith," Ray excitably responded, loading the bun toaster. "We've got plenty of fans. The ceiling fan works just fine. So does the fan over the door."

"Come on, Ray, spend some that hard-earned money on your customers," was Keith's rejoinder. He knew just what buttons to push. He knew Ray had a temper and, knew when he had Ray close to his boiling point.

Ray looked across at Keith and his three employees and yelled, "I'm not buying an air-conditioner for a lousy two weeks out of the year. Now drop it, damn it!"

Keith just laughed as he finished his lunch. As he and his workers walked out of the malt shop, he noticed young Tommy and Lady sharing an ice cream under one of the service windows.

Now that his wife, Mary Ann, had announced she was pregnant, Keith began taking more notice of children. He was thrilled with the prospect of becoming a father. The fact was he craved to be a good father, like his father had been.

"Hey, there young fellow," he said to Tommy as he waved his three employees towards the mechanic shop. "Mighty fine looking dog you have there. What's her name?"

Tommy was busy exchanging licks with Lady when Keith took notice. Lady woofed at Keith but didn't take her eyes off the ice cream cone. When Tommy stopped to answer Keith, Lady took a quick lick.

"Her name's Lady," Tommy answered without looking up. He pushed Lady back. "Quit it!"

Then he looked up to see who asked the question. The man had a heavy mustache, neatly combed; green eyes which sparkled, and a full head of hair perfectly combed. Boots flashed below his mechanics overalls, cowboy-type boots.

"You a cowboy?" Tommy asked looking at the boots.

"I like horses, if that's what you're asking," Keith answered. "Dogs, too," he reached down to pat Lady on the head. "She's a beauty, and she's lovin' that ice cream." Keith stood watching Lady sneak another lick.

Tommy observed Keith's wiry movements and quickness. Keith had a ready smile and friendly way towards Lady. He decided to like the mechanic with the flashy cowboy boots.

"I see you have a leash for Lady," Keith said. "Damn fine leash, too. Kind I use for my dog, Rex."

Taking a lick from the cone, Tommy informed Keith, "My friend, Mr. Truman, said I should get a leash for her. So I did."

Keith stooped over and took the leash in between his fingers and felt it for quality. "I like it," he said to the young boy. "Great color, too. Red."

"Yep, my friend knows stuff," little Tommy said with conviction. Then he added, "He was in The Great War." He paused to let Keith absorb this information. Allowing Lady another slurp of ice cream, he resumed, announcing, "He didn't fight Japs though."

"He didn't?" Keith questioned.

Tommy took another lick of the cone, which was about gone. Keith asked him if he would like another cone. Tommy, thoughtful for a moment, said no, because his mother didn't allow him to take stuff from strangers.

With that, Keith straightened back up and said, "Well, that's good. Listen, I need to get back to work. I'm going to be a Dad soon. I just wanted to say hi and meet your dog. Love your dog. Take good care of her."

"I will," Tommy answered. "Now that I have her leash, it will be safer for her. I'm training her to stay out of the street."

"Good for you," Keith waved back as he was leaving to return to work. "Take care."

Tommy watched the man cross Randolph and vanish through his shop door as Lady took the last bite of cone.

"Come on, girl, we better go home," Tommy said as he stood to leave. Taking care to place his hand through the loop of the leash, he and Lady started off down the sidewalk, she towards the street, he gently pulled her back and called to her, saying, "Come on, girl, stay on the sidewalk. Stay with me." Then firmly but adorned with frustrated love, he commanded, "Stay out of the street."

* * * * * *

It was still weeks before Labor Day and Tommy would be starting school this next school year, the Monday after Labor Day to be exact. He and Lady had still had many more days of playing and going to the malt shop. Many customers at the shop had noticed the boy and his dog. Most stopped to watch them share their vanilla ice cream cone.

Lady was truly a great dog. She showed little of her feral past, wanting to nothing more than be accepted into Tommy's family. When Tommy's Dad carried her into the house that first night last spring and placed her on the kitchen floor in front of Tommy, he remarked, "What a lady she is." For Tommy, it was love at first sight.

Lady scrutinized Tommy for a long moment. Deep from her antiquity—caution at first. She sniffed the youthful boy and sensed he was no danger. Her large round eyes watched him carefully. Seeing he was young, innocent and safe, she bounded into his lap as he sat on the floor encouraging her over and over to "Come, girl."

Her short, stubby tail twitched like the wings of a humming bird, her warm brown eyes watched his every move. She looked up at him from under his chin, caressing his

chin with her cold, black nose. The dateless eons of heredity signaled her, this boy was no threat, this boy could be trusted, and this boy would provide her food and water and companionship. The link between man and dog once again re-affirmed; her sense of enlightenment was handed down from the generations — from the ancient den of gray wolves.
Tommy's parents watched as the union took place, both having had smiles on their lips and warmth in their hearts.

Dad reached for mom's hand and squeezed it gently as they watched the new dog crawl onto their son's lap. Each knew it was a good thing for their son. Dad knew they would play together, endlessly, and that Tommy would learn responsibility. Mom maternally shifted to the needs of the dog, now that it was family.

"Did you bring any dog food?" she asked her husband of ten years. Yes, he answered as he headed back to the garage.

Returning from the garage and the trunk of the car, he brought a case of dog food, two bowls, one for the food, the other, for water. Dad would make it Tommy's responsibility to provide water, and food, to the dog. And, lastly a leash, a nice, new red leash to match the dog's red collar, which coalesced with the young dog's liver colored fur; fur that belied her part American Spaniel heredity.

Coming back with the assortment of canine gear, Dad called out, "Tommy, where are you?"

"We're right here, Dad," Tommy answered as he re-entered the kitchen with the pup following him. Dad showed Tommy the dog's dishes and food. He explained how Tommy would be responsible for the care of his dog. "Tim, you need to give her fresh water daily, sometimes a couple of times," Dad simplified for him. "Feed, her once a day," his Dad then added, "Before school, maybe?"

"We have to think of a name," Mom interrupted as she turned from the kitchen sink where she had been peeling carrots for that night's dinner. Then, declared firmly, "A nice name!" Tommy's Dad looked at her, then smiled and asked, "What's wrong with Dog?" Seeing both Tommy and Mom recoiled at the suggestion as he laughed heartily. "Just kidding," he confessed.

"I already have a name for her—Lady," Tommy said simply. And, with that he bent down and picked Lady up and gave her a hug. "Lady, it's a perfect name for you because you are a little lady."

Mom and Dad looked at each other, both were beaming at the choice, and the fact their son came up with a fitting name on his own. Neither realized it had been Dad's first remark when he first walked in with the cute dog.

And, a Lady she was.

She and Tommy became inseparable—they got up together, ate together, played the summer days away together, and went to bed together with Lady curling up on atop of the bed covers at Tommy's feet. Her canine instincts had been correct. She and Tommy were a pack. Each passing day they spent together their bond strengthened, it including the sharing of an ice cream cone or two down at the corner malt shop, which she had come to expect.

Lady arrival was at the beginning of spring when the Johnny-Jump-Ups were in full bloom, along with their larger cousins, the pansies. Centuries old rituals of spring blooming would repeat until the heat of summer hit. Bulb plants had sprouted. Hyacinths, whose roots go back to ancient Greece, displayed their dense spikes of flowers, fragrant as always and purple, the color of a dense wine. Mom's garden included Tulips, daffodils, and narcissus. The tulips' strong, cup shaped blooms in yellows, whites, reds, pinks covered the beds in Lady and Tommy's backyard.

In one corner, a gazebo stood beside a stately cherry tree, its diminutive blooms pink and full, each perfectly made and colored ever so tenderly. Under the picturesque tree was a row of yellow day-lilies that would bloom many days after the briefly-lived cherry blossoms dropped to the ground; their short cycle echoing the shortness of life. To the antiquated Japanese, cherry blossoms mimic human lives. To a Shinto, life is far too short, but beautiful in its perfection.

Lady and Tommy would often escape under the cherry tree. Here, they would be transported to a delicate, pink world—a world devoid of tension and expectation. It was a world just of Lady and Tommy; together in the harmony and concord of each other's presence. Here, they played in their imaginary world.

Inaudible, unfailingly, spring transformed into summer, its heat quickly taking hold. Still Lady and Tommy romped and played together in their yard, every day. They would take cooling water drinks from the water spigot. Tommy would share his glass of ice water with Lady. She would lap the water furiously to replace the heat collect in her growing body, wagging her tail rapidly as she struck her muzzle into the glass.

Almost daily, Tommy took Lady for an ice cream cone at the malt shop. Since his talk with Mr. Truman, Tommy always had his canine friend on the fire-engine-red leash. The leash had become his teaching tool—his tool to train Lady not to go into the street; for her to walk calmly at his side. He loved the way that Lady walked, pranced was more like it, next to his feet.

Many of the customers looked forward to seeing young Tommy and Lady sitting closely together under one of the walk-up service windows. Each exchanging licks of a vanilla cone. And, as summer moved into fall, Keith, the mechanic, became a fast and true friend of theirs. Tommy liked that

Keith took the time to speak with them, occasionally sat with them, while enjoying his own ice cream cone. Lady was always timid around Keith until the time he offered her a lick of his cone.

She looked at the cone, then at Tommy, who said, "It's OK, girl, have a lick." Lady took a quick lick, then, glanced nervously at her master, did a quick circle and pushed in closer to Tommy.

Keith, while not saying anything, noted Lady's uneasiness while taking a lick off his cone. She was glad she did it, but far gladder when it was over.

"Summers about over, Tommy," Keith asked, "When do you start school?"

Tommy thought for a moment, then, excitedly answered, "Monday. I have all my school stuff. Mom and I got the school stuff yesterday."

"What grade will you be?" Keith asked.

"Kindergarden," Tommy replied, making the name sound like a garden. Keith didn't seem to notice.

"Will you be taking Lady?" Keith questioned with a mischievous smile on his face.

"Oh, no," replied a serious Tommy. Then sadly, he added, "Mom says Lady has to stay home."

Keith sat for a moment, then, said, "Lady will be alright until you get home."

"I hope so," replied a concerned Tommy. He added, "Mom makes Lady stay outside, in the backyard. I worry about her getting out."

Finishing his ice cream cone, Keith stood-up and teasingly said, "You're dog won't get out, nor your mom, either!" Then he ruffled Lady's head roughly and added, "Gotta get back to work. You guys take care." He then turned and raced across the street, stopping at his big mechanic's door, he turned to wave before disappearing inside.

Tommy watch Keith run across the street, then patted Lady on the head, saying, "We better head home, girl. Wonder what he meant about Mom not getting out?"

* * * * *

Early in afternoon the Monday following, Tommy and his mother came home from the first day of kindergarten. He couldn't wait to tell Lady all about school. When they pulled into the driveway, Tommy dashed down the walkway along the north side of the house leading to the backyard. He raced to the gate, released the latch and entered the yard with a holler, "Lady, I'm home!" He ran to the middle of the yard, stopped and looked around for Lady. "Lady, here girl!" he called. No Lady. Again, again, and again he called out for her. No Lady appeared. Tommy's heart quivered. He called again. Still nothing! The yard was quiet. He got that feeling of isolation, the one when one's expectation without provocation is contrary to one's anticipation.

"Lady!" he yelped. "Here, girl." He waited, then yelped again, "Here, girl!" And he waited, and waited. Nothing. Slowly they welded up, in the corner of his eyes, tears.

Mom came through the back gate, closed it, and headed for the backdoor. When Tommy saw her, he screamed, "Ladies not here! What did you do with her? You've lost her!" He ran at his Mom crying hysterically with an overwhelmingly sense of frustration.

"Tommy," Mom said, "calm down, we'll find her. She must be in the yard somewhere." She thought for moment, then, ordered, "Tommy, go look back behind the old chicken coop of your Dad's."

"Where?" Tommy cried out. "Where? Where? Oh, the chicken coup," and he dashed off instantly.

"Tommy," Mom called as he hurried to the old coop, "quit the crying. We will find her." But by the time she said it all, Tommy had run over into the chicken coup area. They were located just behind his Dad's tool sheds. The area was cover with a large tree making it seem a separate world from his and Lady's yard. Tommy never liked the area because in the middle of the coup was the chopping block. Too many chickens had lost their heads there.

He looked quickly around; no Lady. "She's not here," he yelled! "She's not here!" He was looking around desperately when he spotted it. It made his heart sink. Oh, no, it can't be, he thought to himself.

Mom came around the corner of the tool sheds to an anguished Tommy crying and pointing, "Look!"

His mother looked to where Tommy was pointing. There, under the white gingham fence was a shallow indentation, one just big enough for Lady to slip under the fence.

"Mom, she's run away," Tommy whimpered. He added, "I told you, you needed to keep her in the house." He began deep sobs, sobs of a five year old trying to understand what had happened. What to do, he thought bewildered, what to do?

"Tommy, go look around the front yard," Mom commanded. "Check the front porch. If she's not there then wait for me in the car. We'll go looking for her."

It was a most terrible search, driving slowly up and down the neighborhood streets, Tommy at his window shouting out for Lady. "Lady, here girl," he would cry out. Nothing was found of her, then they turned north on to Wilcox. Two blocks down it crossed Randolph. There it had happened.

* * * * *

Tommy's mother had come to what her son called his "cowboy bedroom." Knotty pine was halfway up each wall of the small bedroom. The top portion of each wall was covered with a wallpaper depicting cowboys riding bucking broncos, and covered wagons tracking over wild plains. In one corner there was a large closet for his clothes plus shelves for his many toy trucks, military tanks, and Lionel Trains. His favorite train was the Texas Special. He and Lady loved this room. They had spent hours here.

"Tommy, Mr. Truman is here to see you," Mom said quietly as she looked at her morose son lying on his western quilt.

"Well, I don't want to see him," he retorted, choking back tears. He buried his head in his pillow and began to cry, again. It was the innocent cry of a person not knowing how to face a great reality of life, death. His first death.

Gently, Mom sat on his bed and stroked the back of head and said, "I know, but Mr. Truman made a special trip to see you." With this said, Tommy unhurriedly began his first longest-walk towards dealing with his first loss.

Wiping his eyes as he came into the living room, he sucked in air through lips wet from tears and a nose wet with rivulets of anguish and grief. "Hi, Mr. Truman," Tommy said quietly, torment and pain apparent.

Old Mr. Truman, sitting on the couch, tight and uncomfortable with his mission, acknowledged the sad little boy. He took his cane and drew little circles on the rug in front of the Chesterfield divan, thinking back to a time when, as a young man, he had faced Freddie Falco's parents, so long ago. This didn't aspire to the heights of that loss, but it was close. The old man was uneasy.

"Tommy," Mr. Truman started. "I don't kn ..."

In anguish, Tommy interrupted and blurted out, "You said if I trained her on the leash, she would learn and be OK."

"Yes, but ...," the old warrior tried to say, but Tommy cut him off again.

"You lied," Tommy cried out, sobbing uncontrollably. "Lied, lied, lied!" He darted over to the old man and screamed, "Why did you say that!"

Surprise, the old-timer looked up from the imaginary little circles and answered, "Because it was the right thing to do. Lady did need her leash." He waited a moment for what he said to sink into Tommy's brain and for the young boy to compose himself. Then he added, "Keith did everything he could for her, including rushing her to the veterinary. She was hurt too badly." He paused a moment, giving Tommy time to digest this latest news. Apparently, Tommy wasn't told Keith was the driver who had run over Lady on his way back from delivering a customer's car.

Tommy looked at Mr. Truman perplexed, then, asked, "Our friend, Keith, killed Lady? The mechanic guy who wears cowboy boots? Oh, no. Oh." This was more than young Tommy could understand; he sank to the floor and stared anguished, eyes overflowing with tears.

"How could he do this?" he asked to no one in particular. His young mind was trying to understand, trying to cope with the unthinkable, and trying to deal with improbable. Keith? Keith? "Why would Keith do this? He's our friend. He loved Lady," he asked of Mr. Truman. "He bought her ice cream."

As a man-of-arms, Mr. Truman had had to deal with reality. As a teacher later in life, he always made his students deal with reality. Now he saw it was about reality, again. He said gently to young Tommy, "Tommy, listen to me carefully. Keith did love Lady. Accidents happen. He didn't mean to hurt Lady. It was an accident." He paused a moment, then, went on, "Lady ran out into the street to avoid some people who scared her. She didn't see Keith's car and she ran right in front of it. There was nothing he could do."

Tommy sat there for a moment, thinking. Then, saying with certainty, "It was my fault. I should have never taken her to the malt shop for ice cream." He began to cry again, saying over and over, "It was my fault."

"Tommy," Mr. Truman said, putting a hand under the young boy's chin and raising it in earnest, "Listen to me. It's not your fault. You did all the right things." He paused, then, continued, "When I said she needed a leash, you started using one. When you walked to and from the malt shop, you used the leash to train her to stay out of the street. Tommy, you did all the right things."

Tommy sat grimly for a moment, then, morosely, stated, "Yeah, but Lady's still dead." With that he started to cry again, seared with the pain of his first love lost; pain because a friend, Keith, seemed to be the person guilty for this loss.

For what seemed like hours to Mr. Truman, he sat while his young friend grieved, he patted the anguished young boy's shoulder. Finally, he said, "Young man, we've all had things, bad things, happen to us after we did what we thought were all the right things."

Mr. Truman's mind wandered back to a day at the River Somme, a great battle where his friend Freddie was killed. It was a moment etched into the very fabric of Mr. Truman, a moment when he suddenly realized when you think you've done all the right things, the world may have a different plan for you. Adoration — war metals — coming home — never erased the pain of that day so long, long ago.

Mr. Truman suddenly became aware of Tommy looking at him.

He had quit crying, his red eyes questioning, looking for answers. He finally snickered, "Was it against the Japs?"

The Breakup

The Jade Tree was an oriental restaurant located downtown until the record setting snowfall in the winter of '88. That year Yakima got huge amounts of heavy, wet snow, snow that collapsed over seventy buildings. Jade Tree was one of them.

It was always good, always crowded, and always friendly. The restaurant had lots of regular customers and many out-of-town tourists. The eggrolls, made fresh daily, were delightful and scrumptious. The egg flower soup was always in demand, but Hot N' Sour soup was never offered.

The décor was set in Far-Eastern traditional with gold decorative screens of oriental scenes and Kanji characters surrounding the dining area. O'Bon lamps sat tastefully in corners of high back booths. Each lamp had a Kanji character on its brown rice paper shade and gently lit by a small electric bulb. Each booth had red leatherbacks with flower brocade seats that the staff cleaned nightly.

In one such booth sat old James Austin and his younger wife. With them are her three children by previous marriages, it matters little to James that each child had a different father. The Austins come almost every Friday night, although not always with the kids.

Two booths down is the chief of police and the city mayor discussing the growing gang problem in town. Their wives sit across from each other and talked of the latest scandal to hit town — something about the vice-mayor and one of the council members.

When you walked into the restaurant, George or Kim would greet you with a warm smile and a loud hello. No one was sure of Kim's gender, but Kim had a great smile with a friendly, engaging personality. A buff male customer always got a little extra in the way of a greeting when Kim was welcoming customers to the restaurant.

George, he ran the bar, which was located just off the dining room and when George was bartending (which was most of the time); there was always a good size crowd. At one end of the bar sits the loud and obnoxious Wendell Simon, his grog blossom nose was its usual purple and his cheeks red with purple veins running everywhere on his face. He smoked one cigarette after another and downed the whiskey as if it was soda pop. He banged his empty glass and ordered George to refill it immediately. It didn't matter to George, because Wendell is the largest fruit grower in the valley. Wendell is not George's favorite.

Friday evening was always the busiest evening of the week and this particular Friday is no exception. When Hillary arrived, she looked around the small waiting area but could not spot her friend, Phoebe, whom she is meeting for dinner. In fact, Cole is meeting them both for dinner, together, to catch-up.

Hillary, Phoebe, and Cole have been good friends for years. They practically grew up together. Hillary has not seen Cole for a few weeks, not since they spent the afternoon at her apartment—just the two of them. She blushed when she thought of all that had gone on between them and had hoped he would have been around sooner. He had called and text-messaged a few times, but each time saying work and study was really keeping him busy.

"Phoebe!" she calls out, seeing her friend exiting from the bar. "Is Cole with you?"

"Hey," Phoebe greeted her friend. "No, he just texted me to say he was running a little late. "How are you? God, love that dress. Where'd you get it?"

Hillary was disappointed about Cole but did not show it and decided to enjoy some free moments with Phoebe, who was capable of talking for hours. With a proud smile, she said, "Found it at TJ Maxx, seven dollars. Wouldn't know would you?"

"Its sooo cute," Phoebe said with superficial envy, stretching out the answer.

"Did you get a reservation?" Hillary asks as she looks around the restaurant to see if any booths are empty.

"No," Phoebe answers but points to a table with four chairs. "Grab that table. Oh, oh, hurry before those people see it."

Hillary, being quick, moved quickly to the table and sat down. Turning to her friend, "Got it. And, I can see the front when Cole comes in. How long did he say he'd be?"

Phoebe was busy seating herself. "You know him; he'll be here when he gets here." Deciding to change the subject, she asks, "What have you been doing? We haven't seen each other forever."

"Been busy working. Bunch of weddings coming up, everybody is getting married," she laughs, thinks a moment, then adds, "except for you and me." Hillary has been doing wedding photography for three years. She just opened her first studio.

"Hey, I'm in no hurry," Phoebe answers with a flippant attitude. "Are you seeing anyone special?" she asks her friend.

"No, not since Bernie," Hillary answers, thinking it was two years ago she caught Bernie out with another woman?

"How's about you?" she asks, looking over Phoebe's shoulder to see if Cole has arrived. Where is he, she thinks to herself. Then aloud, adds, "You with anyone special?" She is studying the menu now and fidgeting with her spoon nervously.

Phoebe is staring at the drink menu wondering what to have, then asks, "Are you going to have a drink?"

Hillary likes Margaritas and decides to order one with a double shot of tequila. Phoebe does the same but keeps it to a single shot. As the server starts to walk away, she stops and looks at Hillary intensely, then asks, "Aren't you the photographer that did the Whitman wedding?"

Hillary, leaning a little to the right so she can see the front entrance of the dining room, answers, "Yes, yes, I did do that wedding." Knowing the server will want a card, she reaches in her purse as she continues to watch the entrance and pulls out one of her business cards and hands it to her.

The server looks momentarily at the card and then shoves it into her apron pocket. "I'll be back with your drink order in a few," she said, hoping they would get the hint to order their dinner.

"Where do you think he is?" Hillary asks in a hushed voice, leaning across the table. She checks the entrance area again, but no Cole. Angrily, she unfolds her napkin and whips it across her lap.

"Hillary, he'll be here soon. You must really be hungry," Phoebe, answers with a matter of fact attitude, "I could eat."

The drinks arrive a few minutes later and each take a long, slow pull of their Margaritas.

They told the server that they are waiting for one other person and wish to wait to order dinner. Of course, the server wants to turn the table as quickly as possible, even though George and Kim do not like customers to be hurried. Slackers, the server thinks, that won't help the tips tonight.

As Hillary and Phoebe enjoy their drinks, the restaurant begins to get crowded; a group of people gathers around the reservation desk hoping Kim will be able to get them seated soon. Kim, in a tan leisure suit with a bright yellow flower lay across the shoulders, is entertaining the guests with stories of their last trip to Hawaii.

Kim and George go every year in February and stay two to three weeks, depending on how busy George feels the restaurant has been. George also keeps track of the regulars who come in and if it seems the regulars have not been coming in, he will cut the trip short and return immediately.

"Phoebe, you didn't answer my question," Hillary accuses her friend. "Who are you seeing?"

Phoebe thinks a moment, then says, "No one, really." Hillary looks across the table at her friend with suspicion, and says, "You're lying. You can tell me when I come back." She pushes back her chair and leaves for the restroom.

Hillary brushes by the group at the reservation desk, on her way to the restroom, but really, she is looking for Cole who is still running late. Hillary glances out the glass front doors, no Cole. She looks down the short hallway that leads to the restrooms, no Cole. Into the woman's restroom she goes, then quickly returns to the table. On the way she checks the bar, no Cole. She checks the waiting area, no Cole. She checks the front foyer, no Cole.

"Where can he be," she asks, sitting back down at the table with Phoebe. She moved her two empty Margarita glasses to the edge of table and picks up her third in disgust.

"Hillary, chill," Phoebe answers, sipping her second Margarita. "Besides, he probably got delayed by Megan."

Hillary froze for a moment. Her large, mysterious brown eyes narrowed as she asks, "Who the hell is Megan?" Just as she said that, she saw Cold move quickly through the front doors and scan the restaurant.

Phoebe leaned across the table to impart confidential information, having had enough margaritas, and said, "He didn't want me to say anything, but I can tell you. Besides, I've had enough to drink. It's his new girlfriend; been going together for a couple of months, now."

"A couple of months," Hillary repeated, thinking of what happened in her apartment three weeks ago. She looked up to the reservation desk and saw Kim pointing to their table and directing Cole how to get there.

Cole, arriving at their table gave out a bellicose, "Hey, hey, hey. What's happening?"

Phoebe, boozed-up and getting syrupy, stood and gave Cole a warming hug, pushed back a little and said laughing, "Finally, you have arrived. I could not have another margarita. Jesus, I'm feeling the first-two." She swayed a little side to side, but her eyes danced with joy to see her friend. She and Cole had been friends since grammar school, all through high school, even went to the same college, Central Washington.

Hillary sat there. She watched the two of them greet each other with warmth and familiarity. Cole was jubilant. Phoebe was euphoric, and drunk. Hillary was livid. She was thinking, two months ago, and the heat built. "Three weeks ago," she thought and the heat built more. His lateness because of Megan, and the heat really built. Her eyes were fuming, her expression, furious. Her tongue would become a whip, snapping blows at him and making him walk the walk of shame. "The bastard!" she screamed to herself.

Finally, he turned to Hillary saying, "Hey, there. How are you?" He started to bend over and give her a hug when she pushed him back and stared at him with venomous eyes, ready to exterminate the rat.

"Don't bother," she said under her breath. All could see she was extremely uncomfortable, like an animal trying to escape. Cole backed off, seeing that she was upset, and gave her a big, "Well, hello."

Phoebe had sat back down and was looking at the menu. She said that now everyone was here, at last, everyone could finally order. Cole said he wanted a beer, a Corona with lime he called to a passing waiter.

"A beer," Hillary questioned? "Why would you want a beer with me? Why don't you go have a beer with your new friend?"

Phoebe looked up and over her menu, not sure what she had just heard. She looked over at Cole who had a big, condescending smile as he studied the dinner menu. Apparently, he had not heard the same thing that Phoebe thought she heard. Oh, well, she thought, I must not have heard correctly.

Their server arrived at the table and greeted everyone, wanting to know if they wanted to order more drinks, or dinner, or both? "I asked a waiter for a Corona," Cole replied.

Phoebe and I will be ordering dinner," Hillary said, looking every part the demon from Hell. Like a whip snapping overhead, she said, "He will be leaving." Then coyly, she looked at Cole and said sweetly, "Won't you?" And, before he could answer, she acidly added, "Got to get back to the NEW little woman, I should think."

"I can stay," Cole answered innocently, not sure what he should do. "I came to enjoy your company and Phoebes."

Phoebe, who was very sharp with a camera, but a bit too intoxicated to understand what was happening, hid behind her menu. She reached around the menu and pulled her Margarita into her for a quick swig. "God, what is happening?" she asked herself.

Hillary looked at Cole and snapped, "Really?" She paused for a moment, then, added, "What? You think you can come in here and act like nothing is wrong. That I don't know what you've been doing? You ass, I am fifty steps ahead of you, you bastard!"

"But, Hillary, Honey, I don't want trouble," Cole replied with sincerity. He squirmed a bit in his seat, knowing he's tangled in a lie, yet, not ready to concede. "Honey, I want to be here with you, now."

"You, Bastard, don't you dare call me 'Honey'," Hillary said back to him none to quietly. Her eyes was smoldering, her shoulders tense, her tongue was poised and said, "Get your ass out of here."

The server looked around the table and knew just what to do—she left. Phoebe put down the menu for a second time and looked at each of them. She couldn't figure out what was happening.

"Do I need to go into the bar so you two can be alone," she asked?

"No," they both answered, almost in unison.

Phoebe looked at both of them and asked, "What's going on?"

Hillary was the first to answer, "What is it, Cole? You screw me one day and the next you're out with Megan?"

With a look of the dawn of knowledge, Phoebe said, "Oh, shit."

"It's not like that," Cole protested, looking at Hillary.

"Really, then how is it," Hillary retorted with anger.

"I have feelings for you, Hillary," he genuinely responded, remembering their encounter a few weeks ago.

"Oh, really!" she shot back and then continued, "So you sleep with me three weeks ago, but have been going out with Megan for two months. Slept with her, yet?" Hillary topped for a pause, then, added, "No, she probably smarter than that."

He started to explain, but she cut-in sharply and said, "Get lost, get out of here!"

Phoebe offered, "I better go to the bar."

"No, you don't need to," Hillary said loudly, the drinks were showing, heads were beginning to turn. One mother turned her daughter's head back to their booth and told her not to stare. Other diners were snickering. The women were pissed, the men felt penitent for Cole, yet, understanding. "The poor bastard is caught," they each thought with a giggle.

Phoebe just sat not knowing exactly what she should do next and trying to figure out how she had missed the relationship between Hillary and Cole. She asked Hillary, "How long have you two been an item?"

"Oh, I don't know for sure," Hillary answered questioningly, then looked at Cole with eyes that could kill and said, "You tell us Cole, you ass. Tell Phoebe, two, maybe three years, you, bastard! Too, busy with work right now, and studies. Now's not the time to move the relationship forward?" Hillary jeered. "Let's wait, I think you said?" She looked at Cole with venom, then, looked away in discuss. Finally, "What'cha tell Megan?" she questioned, looking back at Cole, then continued, "I know what you said you two-timing bastard. Nothing!"

Cole sat there, pitiable. Phoebe felt sorry for him. The rest of the restaurant customers were all straining to hear Hillary's latest barrage, but each tried not to look obvious.

"Did you say, 'Oh, Megan, we just need to wait a little longer, I just have so much work and studying to do,' when really you just want to make it with Hillary a few more times." She paused a moment, then questioned, "Sound about right, you two timing bastard?" she hissed across the table at Cole.

Cole had set his cell phone on the table and as Hillary concluded her hissing at him, she quickly reached across the table before Cole realized it. She had grabbed his cell phone in her hot little hand.

"I know," she said like a middle-school girl. "Let's call her and tell her about Hillary, Cole!"

As Hillary flipped the phone open, Cole reached across the table and asked surprised, "What are you doing?" He held out his hand to Hillary and commanded, "Give it back."

She answered by pushing his hand away and saying, "Let's call her and invite her to dinner!" She poked a couple of keys and then said, "Ah, there's the number. Let's see. Cole, how do you make it dial?"

Cole was beet red and getting off his seat, in a hushed tone said, "Give me back my phone. Hillary, quit! You're being silly."

"Silly!" she yelled. "Silly!" She looked around the room, seeing everybody looking, she said so all could hear, "I'm being silly!" "Silly?" she said even louder in a questioning tone.

"Hillary, Chill out," Phoebe injected. "Give Cole the phone."

"Oh, Phoebe says I should give you the phone. Here," She said in a low and goofy voice. "Here's your phone, asshole!" With that she caught a glimpse of a water pitcher sitting on the table and promptly dropped the phone in it, watching as it sank to the bottom with little bubbles coming out of it. "Oops," she giggled.

Everyone in the restaurant was watching, too. Some of the fellows laughed, one woman applauded, another looked at Hillary and mouthed the words, "Way to go, woman." The little girl, who had been staring earlier, looked at the pitch with the phone at the bottom and began to laugh. Her mother, who had reminded her not stare, also busted out laughing. She cupped her mouth and looked at her daughter shaking her head with a giggle.

"Oh, shit," Cole said, reaching his hand into the pitcher to retrieve the phone. "Hillary, you're being stupid, now."

She shot back, "Cole, you're the one being stupid by not leaving."

"Do you know how much I paid for this phone?"

"I don't care, Cole!"

"Six hundred dollars," Cole yelled, not hearing her. "Six-hundred fucking dollars."

"Well, dry it off and let's call Megan to see if it works," Hillary teased. Everyone was laughing. Phoebe just wanted to leave. She signaled for their server but when she arrived, Phoebe ordered another Margarita.

"Another round?" the server asked. Then she questioned, "Hey, Romeo, does the phone work?"

The audience laughed as the serving woman strutted off for Phoebe's drink.

Cole, at this time, called his brother Pete and asked, "Is my voice clear?" He waited for the reply, and then stated, "Hillary accidentally dropped it in a pitcher of water."

"It wasn't an accident, Peter," She said loudly at the phone. "Think I'll have another drink," she added.

"Ok, great, it works," Cole said. "I'll call you later, when we're done with dinner."

Hillary yelled, "Cole's not staying." However, Cole had already folded his phone and put it in his shirt pocket.

Kim appeared at the table to ask in broken English, "What going on here? People, they complain?" Looking around the table, Kim waited for an answer.

"Cole is causing trouble and was just leaving," Hillary volunteered.

Kim looked at Cole, "You cause trouble? How?"

Cole, looking embarrassed, stated, "It's Hillary, she's just a little confused."

"Confused," Hillary cut-in, then looking at Kim, she added, "The two-timing bastard been sleeping with me, but dating someone named Megan." She waited a moment for Kim to absorb the information and then asked, "What would you do, Kim?"

Kim stood a moment, looking around at the other patrons, seemingly uncomfortable. She asked Cole, "You two-timer?"

Cole was about to answer when his cell phone began its merry little tune. With relief, he pulled his phone out and said loudly, "Hello."

"Hey," He smiled, turned a bit red, then, added quickly, "What's up?" Suddenly, he stood up and turned his back on the others. "Oh God, sure, I'll be right there." He hung up the phone and as he turned slowly around, he reached for his wallet.

"What do I owe, I need to leave?" he said rapidly and deliberately. "Kim, get my bill?"

"Kim, just get the bastard his bill. Phoebe and I are staying for a nice dinner without this two-timer." She looked at Cole and snidely asked, "Little woman call? Have to hurry."

Looking at Cole, Kim said, "Seven dollar, then you go. Is good?"

Cole handed Kim a ten and said to keep the change. "No, not good, I need to get going," he said, looking at Phoebe.

"Is everything OK?" Phoebe asked, sensing Cole seemed tense about the call.

"Oh, don't be concerned with the bastard, Phoebe," Hillary said coldly.

"What is it, Cole?" Phoebe asked, again. "Is something wrong?"

"It's Megan," Cole said. He looked at Hillary, then, turned to Phoebe and said, "She just found out that her father was killed in a car accident a couple of hours ago."

Richardson Park

She sat crying. Big tears, heavy tears, tears containing no hope, tears of despair, tears of one whose heart's been broken by life. Her sobs were genuine; her shoulders were shaking as she reached to wipe her nose. She dried her eyes, then, took a deep breath in a vain attempt to collect herself before more tears emerged from those oval brown eyes. The brown mascara streaked down her reddened, plump cheeks. Weighty tears, gloomy ones at best, cascaded again as she attempted to gather herself, but to no avail.

And, through the mist, he watched.

Richardson Park is not a public park. It does not sit in the middle of a city, or of a town. It's not a park where people take their children, or their grandchildren. It is definitely not a big park, but a pretty one? Yes.

This park sits at the entrance to the Estates. Not big estates, but, rather, small estates made up of mobile homes with nice yards. These are estates of people who didn't necessarily make the grand grade of success in life. Some got a bad break; others took risks and fell short. Many just got too old trying. Most are just hanging-on, living off government doles that barely meet the standard of a livable wage.

Sarah was seated on the sole park bench, struggling with her latest difficulty in her young life. The teenager's discomfort was genuine, maybe, even disingenuous.

And still, he watched.

Sitting there, she looked vacantly at the tall row of arborvitae shrubs bordered by the beautiful blooming hydrangeas at their feet. The blue and pink blooms were huge in size, great in character, balanced in their circular shape.

In between the hydrangeas are rhododendrons, nice ones that had bloomed earlier in the spring in grand clusters of purple and whites.

Along the front of the blooming hydrangeas lies a collection of many bright, green-leafed hostas with creamy-white margins. A few having large, deep green leafs with well-defined rivulets. They're known as Big Toms.

Over in one corner of this mottled landscape struggles an ugly orphan, a hostas with its creamy margins eaten away by earwigs and slugs. Its once proud leafs droopy and spent. Life has been hard on it, but it continues to skirmish with life.

Sarah's eyes fixed upon the poor specimen. She understood having the world eat away at one's self. In her mind, it echoed over and over, the cruelties of her "friends." To her very face they applied the words, "fat and ugly," "fat and ugly," "fat and ugly." Behind her back more of the same. Over and over, she repeats the words. Over and over, she tried to comprehend. Over and over, she repeated words, then, just wanted to die. On the park bench, she sits there, sobbing and crying.

Then, slowly, through the mist, he approached.

In a low, guttural voice, Sarah said, "Maybe I should just kill myself." The sentence hung out there. He heard it. It startled him. Then, settling unnoticed on the opposite end of the park bench, he asked aloud gently, "Did I just hear what I thought I heard?"

His question made Sarah jump. She hadn't realized anyone was around to hear her comments. Looking at the stranger, Sarah blurted, "Who're you?"

The man who sat on the bench next to her was an older man, much older. His hair was thin, gray and wispy, but neatly combed, combed back over a balding spot on the crown of his head. His forehead was receding. He had a pallor look about him.

"My name's Noah," he answered quietly. He waited a moment, then, added, "And, I heard what you said. Why?" He waited for an answer.

"It's really none of your business," she answered brusquely.

He just sat there staring, saying nothing. It seemed he was looking through her or maybe he was staring deep into her soul. He stood for a moment while he brushed off maple leaves that had floated down on him.

Resuming his position on the bench, he said, "I know, but it makes me nervous when a young, beautiful person talks about killing herself." He spoke quietly but his words and demeanor bore weight. He sat waiting.

Sarah cried a bit.

Shifting her corpulent body, finally she sniveled, "First of all, I'm not beautiful." She sucked in a gulp of air, blew her nose uncaringly, and brushed back her curly hair before adding, "Have you looked at me? Really looked at me?"

"Not really. This is the first time we've met, but you're beautiful to me," Noah responded. He waited a moment then added, "What makes you think you're not petty?"

"My family," as she descended into despair. "My brother and sister have always said it. They always tell me how fat I am. My Dad, too! He thinks I'm too fat."

"Do you think you're fat?" Noah questioned. Then without thinking, loudly he blurted, "Your Dad!"

The bulky girl just sat. Sitting like a long-suffering person, she whispered, "Yes, my father."

The man sat there, not moving, not seeing, but lost deep in thought. He lingered a moment over his relationship with his father, then, decided this young lady was misunderstanding hers. He told her so, but she was determined.

"I know what he said to me," she answered.

Then she took her cell phone out, punched a few buttons, and leaned over to show him the screen.

Looking at the screen, he couldn't believe what he was reading. He quickly grabbed the phone and held it close to his face. The glare from the device's screen made his face seem even whiter than it actually was. *You Bitch, I don't want you anymore, you're too fat*, it stated, jumping off the screen and burning into his consciousness.

He re-read the message a second time, then a third time. Try as he might, he couldn't comprehend a father saying this to his child. The implications were enormous, huge, and considerable. Even significant, but in the end, it saddens him.

He thought, "What harm some parents do to their children."

"What does the rest of your family say?" Noah questioned aloud. He waited for a moment while Sarah struggled with the question, then, he pushed, "Do you have brothers or sisters who can help?"

The questions seem to add to her misery. With a wretchedness, and desolation, she struggled with herself, trying to form words through the tears. Finally, she just shook her head and with despair, distress and agony. She answered quietly, "They don't care."

As she says this, he slides along the bench towards her, coming within an arm's length.

The distraught girl's head sagged as he tried to look directly into her red, teary eyes. He unequivocally questioned, "Come on, surely, they care?"

"No—they don't," she stated with a despondency full of loneliness. She thought for a moment, then, finally she just shook her head in despair and said, "No, they don't." She looked away wiping more new tears away.

"Surely, your mother?" he pushed her further.

She thought back over time, a short time ago, then, long ago. She couldn't think of a time when Mom came to her rescue. She remembered a morning not so long ago when Dad had left her room. She had gone down stairs. Mom was there, huddled in a corner, crying. When she saw her mom crying, she, too, started to cry. She started to console her mother, but mom refused her overtures. Instead, mom ordered her to get to the table and eat her breakfast. As she slid into her place at the table, Dad appeared in the doorway. Tension filled the air. Mom left the room, Dad sat down. Sarah's brother joined them. The tension lessened.

"Mom had her own problems," Sarah had replied to Noah.

"Like what?"

Blankly she stares across the park, struggling to find the words to answer the question.

Then simply, quietly she responded, "She drinks, does drugs. Just recently I saw her using a needle. You know, like the doctor uses." She paused a moment, then continued, "I think she's doing heroin."

"The truth is," she explained to Noah, "she can't help me because she has her own bad problems."

"She's an addict," Sarah pronounced with conviction. "An addict," she repeated.

"She can't help me, just like I can't help her." Anger crossed her face, transient but apparent. "What can she do for me?"

Noah sat a moment, thinking, then, posed a question, "Maybe you should be asking what you can do for her?"

"Do for her?" Sarah questioned. A moment later, she added, "I can't do anything for her. I've tried and all she does is pushes me away."

She explained to Noah how much her mother has yelled at her, pushed her away and told her to get lost. "She doesn't want my help, Noah," she spit out between tears.

There was another long pause. Toiling with pain, Sarah added, "She told me to get lost. She doesn't want me."

The pain was almost too much as she thrashed about for her next statement. "She told me to go kill myself," Sarah finally said crying.

Noah sat silently, listening, unsure what to say.

"My own mother," Sarah cried. "My own mother tells me to go kill myself." In disbelief, she again repeated, "My own mother.

"From the beginning, I don't remember her paying attention to me. She never worried about the typical mom stuff. I don't think she knows what typical moms are supposed to do."

Quietly Noah stood, again brushing more leaves off, not sure what to say, not sure what to do. He considered leaving. This was too much for him. He looked around the park hoping someone else would wander in and take over this burden. He looked at Sarah sitting on the park bench with a heavy heart. In her face he sees the despair, the look of isolation and intense depression. He struggles with the situation, but he knows she can't be left like this.

Sitting back down on the bench, he asked Sarah, "Are you and your sister, or brother, close?"

The older teen was quick to answer. "Not really," she retorted. "She has a boyfriend, such as he is."

Her face goes blank as she considers her sister's situation. Her expression told Noah not to push.

But Noah did push. He asked, "Such as he is? What does that mean?"

"It means he is worthless," Sarah replied with bitterness. "He claims to love my sister, but he doesn't! He's too busy trying to make it with me."

She shivered at the thought. Because of that, it made her sister to not want her around.

"Have you told your sister," Noah asked?

"Tell her what? She wouldn't believe me. Besides, she blamed me for it. I did try once and all she did was blame and call me a fat ass. It was terrible. Until then I thought my sister and I were close. Guess, not." She wiped her eyes, blew her nose, and then sat there morosely as the morning mist thickened.

"Your sister is older?" he asked.

"Yes. By a year," the pudgy girl answered. "She's nineteen."

The old man thought for a moment. He shifted a bit on the bench then said, "Sounds like her first real romance?" As he saw Sarah nod in agreement, he added, "It's natural for a young girl in her first romance to be touchy about it. Maybe you're being too touchy."

A low sigh from Sarah was followed by, "Maybe." She sits there, lost in thought.

An early morning jogger in black sweats came trotting by. The runner was a lady in her older fifties. She had a beautiful black, huge Great Dane with an upright tail, loping at her side. Neither runner nor dog seemed to notice the two people on the bench. Quietly, they disappeared amongst the gray morning mist.

Noah watched as they faded into ghost like figures, then, evaporated. They appeared to have dissolved into the dreary mist. For a moment, the pair had felt familiar then he turned his attention back to Sarah.

Sarah was twirling her auburn hair over and over through her fingers, nervous about what to do next. Finally she said, "I don't know what to do." Studying her for a moment, the old man suddenly suggested, "Get a dog!"

"A dog," she repeated. Her face brightens a bit before saying, "I already have a dog ... Chloe"

"Chloe is your dog?"

Sarah started fiddling with her cell phone, then leaned across to Noah and showed him a picture of a little black dog with a white leg.

"That's Chloe," she stated with new-found joy.

She and Noah both looked at the picture of her dog. Sarah entire demeanor was suddenly jubilant and joyous. Noah sensed this and was about to say something when Sarah blurted out, "My God, I forgot to feed her."

Suddenly she jumped up and said, "I gotta go, Noah,"

"What about killing you?"

"I don't have time for that," she cracked back as she stood up. "I gotta go feed Chloe."

She stopped and looked at Noah, "If I don't feed Chloe, no one will. I'm all she's got." Leaning over to the old man, Sarah reached out and touched him lightly on the shoulder in a friendly gesture adding, "Thank-you for listening. It was nice."

Noah stood, there confused, "Did we solve anything?"

"Not sure," Sarah answered. "But I feel better. Besides, I have a babysitting interview after school." She took his hand and looked directly into his eyes and said, "Thank you so much for listening."

With that, she turned and began her walk home. As she started to fade into the early morning, she turned one more time to wave and thank the little old man who had listened to her troubles. But when she turned back the park bench was empty. The bench where they sat was cover with fall leaves. She looked about but he's nowhere to be seen.

"Moves kind of fast for an old-fart," she laughed aloud.

* * * * *

The house sat high on the hill, just below the crest. It was a newer house, dark brown. The land spread out from the house making it appear bigger than it actually was. It was a Rambler home, the type cowboys and horse people like.

The living room window was a large, single-pane. People in Southern California called such a large window a "picture window." The picture in this window was of the Cascades. Mt. Adams stood out, but far in the distance. In the foreground were rolling green hills and the fenced-in ranch land that went the house. Two red Roans munched on the prolific green Kentucky Blue grass, swishing their tails as they ate.

It was four o'clock. Sarah sat at the front gate in her age-old Volkswagen with little puffs of blue smoke jettisoning out twin tail pipes. Looking up the long driveway leading to the house, she wondered what she is about to get herself into. She reached out through the window and pushed the button which opened the gate. As it swung open, she gunned the old car through the entry way, leaving a cloud of smoke to envelope the rod iron-gate.

When the front door opened, a lady of much bearing, poise, and age presented herself. She had an inviting smile. She said, "You must be Sarah, come in." Sarah smiled and nodded as the woman opened the door wide and stood to one side and grandly swept her arm, jesting to Sarah to enter. The older woman announced, "I'm Mrs. Richardson."

Sarah entered the house as a large black Great Dane came loping through the spacious living room right up to Sarah. He looked at her a moment then immediately stuck his nose in Sarah's crotch and sniffed.

As Sarah jumped, Mrs. Richardson yelled, "Harley, down!" She buffeted at the huge animal, but to no avail. Harley just buried his head that much deeper and firmer. At last, Sarah twisted away, embarrassed, plus a bit of fear was present.

The older woman exclaimed how sorry she was about the big dog's behavior. As a frivolous excuse, she said, "He's in doggy training."

"Really," Sarah managed to muster, then with a laugh, added, "It's hard to know."

Mrs. Richardson laughed softly, then, answered, "Yes, well I understand how you must feel." She then went on to explain why she needed a babysitter three days a week. "You see my daughter just went to work and wants me to baby sit her three year old," as she motioned for Sarah to follow her.

They went through the expansive living room from which Harley had come, and into the kitchen by way of a family room. The family room had a huge open hearth, like something from the early West. Next to the frontier-style hearth stood a set of bookshelves crowded with family pictures.

The pictures were typical of family photos. There were a lot of horse photos, too. In many of the pictures was a younger Mrs. Richardson. In a couple of the photos was Mrs. Richardson and what looked to be her husband. He was a cowboy-type with an oversized belt-buckle, boots, and a large Montana hat that hid his face in a dark shadow. Sarah studied it a moment. Something was familiar about the man. "Where have I seen him before?" she questioned herself.

Her thought was interrupted by Mrs. Richardson, "Let's sit in the kitchen," she was saying. "Would you like something to drink?"

Sarah turned from the family pictures and walked into a spacious kitchen. In the center was a large kitchen island designed to accommodate six people at a time. At one end of the island were a kitchen sink and a stove. Sarah chose to sit on one of the center stools.

"Boy, it's really hot out," she said, adjusting her girth. "Do you have lemonade?" A beer was closer to what she really wanted, but this was a babysitting interview.

Mrs. Richardson was looking in the refrigerator when she spotted a Coors way in the back. "Noah must have put it there before ...," she thought to herself. Then, to test the young teen at her counter, she stated temptingly, "I have beer."

Immediately, almost too fast, Sarah replied, "Oh no, ma'am, I don't drink."

Mrs. Richardson paused a moment in thought. "You know, I do have some lemonade in here," she said, holding the refrigerator door open. "I'll get it, and then let's talk awhile."

They visited for over an hour, with Mrs. Richardson asking all types of questions. Most were designed to find out what type of person Sarah was. But Sarah answered each question carefully with straightforward replies.

When Mrs. Richardson was satisfied, she told Sarah she needed her Thursday, Friday evenings, plus all day Saturday. If she heard the low groan from Sarah, she didn't let it on. She felt she knew the teenager.

It happened when Sarah was fixing to leave. After getting her final instructions from Mrs. Richardson, she slipped off her stool and turned to go. At that moment a picture caught her attention. It hung there on the wall right by the kitchen door. "Oh, my God," she said with astonishment. "Isn't that Noah?" She moved up close to the picture, looking at it in amazement.

Mrs. Richardson, who was standing by the door said, "Why, yes it is." Then she added, "He was my husband."

Sarah, wanting to impress her new employer said, "He is so nice."

"Nice?" Mrs. Richardson said. She looked confused.

"Yes," replied Sarah. "He listened to all my problems." She thought a second, then, added, "He made me feel a lot better."

"He was always a good listener," Mrs. Richardson said cheerfully. "Where did you get the chance to talk to him dear?"

"Over at the small park inside the Estates," young Sarah replied. She remembered how he had made her feel good, like he was really interested in her. "He's so nice."

Mrs. Richardson, still mildly confused, asked, "And, when was this Sarah?"

Sarah explained how she had been feeling low and depressed. "I was seated on the park bench this morning, early. He kind of came out nowhere and sat with me for an hour or so." She recalled the scene and how Noah had helped her to understand her parents better. "He was great!" she concluded. "Really!" was all Mrs. Richardson could marshal. Then she asked again, "When was this?"

"This morning, early," Sarah replied innocently, "at the park."

"Honey, you must be mistaken," Mrs. Richardson said sadly. "Noah died over a year ago."

Sarah stood there for a moment. She repeated the word, "Died?" Now it was her turn to be confused. "But," she insisted, "We talked this morning, early, in the park. How'd he die?"

Woefully, Mrs. Richardson said quietly, "He committed suicide.

Parody of A Home Coming

The ranch is well run. You can tell that just by looking at it. It is not a large apple ranch by today's standards--forty acres, ten acres in cherries and the remaining acres in various apple varieties.

It sits on the southern exposure of the Diamond Back Ridge alongside the old highway which snakes its way along the valley floor; A antediluvian ranch that someday Allen Rooster and his wife, Catherine, look forward to leaving to their one son, Keith, just as Allen's Dad left it to his son and his Dad before that.

The main house is white with a high, pointed roof of green composition shingles above French doors that open to a large red cement patio covered by a pergola draped with Wisteria. The house has sat above the orchard for over one hundred years. Each window has green shutters. The view is the large expanse of the valley. You can see the river below and Mt. Adams off to the West. The river meanders along the new state highway and in summer, the Cottonwood blooms drift across the road and into the orchard.

The old highway, now known as Wine Country Road, passes by the front of the house and a beautiful lawn that Allen keeps painstakingly groomed and green, separates the two.

An old Willow tree weeps gracefully next to the old road and is the main inhabitant of a yard that has a collection of roses, and lava-rocks, and finely selected perennials. Mrs. Rooster loves this charming old house and its picturesque gardens. She raised their three children here, the two older girls and Keith.

Looking out her kitchen window, "Mother Hen", Keith's pet name for his mother, looks out across the well-groomed lawn to see the yellow school bus stop across the road to discharge its latest load of students. In past years, Keith had been one of those students. "Just three years ago," she thinks to herself. Now he is finishing his first eighteen-month assignment in Iraq. However, tomorrow he would come busting through the front door ahead of Allen, laughing loudly and enfolding her in a big bear hug, saying how good to be home. She could hardly wait.

In his last email, he had said he wanted to celebrate all the holidays that he had missed during the past 18 months. He said it would be his excuse for not doing chores. "Won't be able to do chores if I am celebrating a holiday," he had joked in his email. She had laughed when she read the teasing comment, but lifted an eyebrow in contemplation. "What will Dad think, she had asked? "Prepare for lots of holiday celebrating," he answered back.

She picked up the ringing telephone and was pleased to hear her daughter's voice on the other end. "Mom, it's me," Kathy laughed. "When does Keith arrive home?"

"Hi, Kathy," Mom replied. "According to your father, Keith lands tomorrow at two in the afternoon." She thought to herself that Allen would be at the airport at noon, busting with excitement and anticipation, waiting for his son.

"O.K., we'll be at the house at four. We getting off work early," Kathy explained. "I will be bringing Brea with me." Brea, Keith's girlfriend of the last five years, has been an item since the tenth grade and everyone expects they will marry soon. Brea and Kathy work together at the local Target Store.

"That's great. Keith will be excited to see you both." She thought about all the people who would be stopping by to welcome Keith home and all the work needed done to prepare for the dinner that would take place in the evening.
"Could you bring some chips and sodas?" she asked.

Just as Kathy answered, she heard the doorbell. "Listen, Honey, someone is at the front door," she said looking out the French windows over the kitchen counter. A polished black car with a small emblem that she couldn't make out was parked in the driveway. The doorbell rang a second time. "I better go," she said to Kathy, not wanting to keep any well-wishers waiting.

She got to the front door and before opening the door she straightened her dress, fixed her hair, put on her biggest and best smile. Then she opened the front door.

Standing on the porch were two tall Marines dressed in their formal dress-blues. Their shoes were as polished as the car they came in. They had on their white gloves and white hats and belts with gold buckles, each buckle were highly polished, the red lining of their tunics perfectly aligned. Each took off his hat and placed it under his left arm. Then the taller one spoke, "Mrs. Rooster … ?"

Norma Jean

She was just a wisp of a woman. Small framed, delicate some would say, a strong jaw and eyes that reflected a lifetime of struggle. But she could size you up in a single glance. A small woman, physically, but with warmth and love that grabbed all who met her. Norma Jean did nothing great, she was no news-maker and, in fact, in her wild, younger days she sat on a lot of bar stools.

In those days, she had youth on her side, strong and beautiful, yet, delicate. Men fought over her, just to be at her side and some even tried to tame her wildness. Once she found a man just as wild as her; her girls became a reality. Their births did not slow her flight through life. She still drank and smoked and did pot and slept around. She looked for the next party, the next drink, the next high, the next man. The babies stayed with whomever-nothing slowed her down, not even her girls.

And, as time moved on, which it always does for everyone, the babies grew and became young women. The oldest was spirited and wild like her mother. The younger was quieter and reserve, perhaps, overwhelmed by the two older family "starlets." Nothing, it seemed, would change the family paradigm. Norma Jean would stay wild and uncontrolled, and her oldest would follow in mama's footsteps. Life was one great party and nothing would change.

But, something did change. One day while sitting on a stool, downing one "last-one" for the road, an epiphany took place, which would change Norma Jean-forever. What caused it? No one knows for sure. Maybe it was the realization that her oldest girl was following her example and now at fifteen was as bad as, or worse, than mom had been at that age. Or, maybe "time" had caught up with Norma Jean as time catches up with everyone.

Time is the great equalizer, the great element that cannot be defeated or conquered. Illustrious or small, famous or infamous, time affects everything without regard, without favor and without sentiment. It does not diminish accomplishment, it does not elevate failure; it does bring the great and the small into balance with reality. That reality we call mortality.

Norma Jean for all her wildness, all her partying and all her lack of responsibility did have a mother's instinct for what was good for her girls. Like a wild animal, she sensed what was right for her offspring. She knew the dangers that could bring them down and hurt them. She was too familiar with what life could do to young girls and she was mother enough to know that she wouldn't let that happen to her young. She needed to get them to safety and protect them from the ravages of life. Sitting on a bar stool that day she made the decision that would change all their lives forever.

Simply-she needed to go home. She needed to take the girls to grandma's house. That day she and her girls left and went home.

Home was a small town of no more than 50,000 souls. The main industry was farming which provided the world with apples and soft fruits, like pears, apricots and peaches. Main Avenue bisected First Street in the exact middle of town, both vied for years to be the financial and business center of Yakima. In the end, First Street expanded and Main contracted.

Yakima has its share of churches and schools, along with brothels and bars. There were places called The Alaskan and The Ranch House, where wild-ones could sow their oats and drink their fill. Norma Jean's mother said that she wouldn't allow that around her grandchildren and that kind of stuff would have to stay out of the house. She told her daughter to get a job.

"To be a waitress never killed anybody," she said. "Besides, you need the money." Then she added, "Also, you need to grow up."

Norma Jean struggled with life in those days of waiting tables and finding a bar stool to sit on. Most days after work she would find her way to a bar stool at The Alaskan, leaving it only to go to a really wild party that promised to be the best yet.

Then one day it happened. At this "best yet" party, she was getting her buzz of the day on. Far across the room a guy with thick black glasses and slicked down blond hair combed like a professor, basically a nerd, came across the room and introduced himself. He mumbled and stumbled but did manage to say who he was and asked if he could take her home.

"What, to your house," she had asked?

"No," he replied turning red, "to your house." He paused and, then added, "Maybe we could stop for coffee?"

She couldn't believe it. A Nerd wanted to take her home. She looked him in the eye and said "no" in a voice that would discourage anyone else but a Nerd. Later she disappeared with him.

They had coffee in his car because she was too drunk to walk into a restaurant. Eddie was polite, soft spoken and a gentleman. This was a new experience for Norma Jean. When he dropped her off at her mom's house she didn't invite him in. Thank god that's over, she thought, not remembering she put his phone number in her wallet.

Just in case you need my help, as he handed her his number. A Nerd, oh God, never!

He phoned every night for a week to talk with her, but she had mom tell him she was working. On the seventh straight night, right at eight o'clock the phone rang. Mother said she wasn't going to lie anymore.

"Take the call and be done with it," she told her headstrong daughter.

Norma Jean gave a sigh, picked up the phone and rudely asked, "What do you want?"

He told her in his soft-spoken manner he had been thinking about her and was hoping to take her to dinner sometime.

"No, I don't think we should date," she replied, thinking, not me, not with a geek.

"It wouldn't have to be a date," he responded. "We're just friends."

"Look, you're a nice guy, but you're a geek and I don't date geeks."

Done firmly informing him, she hung-up. Mother just shook her head. She told her mother she had to work, but, instead, left for a party up in the hills at her girlfriend's house.

Later that night, Norma Jean checked her watch. Realizing it was two in the morning, she knew she had to be at work at five! She took a squinted looked at her partner of the evening.

He was the biker type with tattoos, well built, and she had spent most of the night with him. Yet, he couldn't be bothered with driving her home. He had said as much. All he wanted was more of her flesh and she needed to get home to get ready for work. She had her girls to thinks of, but she was drunk on her butt.

Norma Jean knew she needed to get going. Reaching into her wallet she found his number, Eddie's number.

Above the noise, she yelled into the phone she needed a ride home.

"Yeah, it's really two-thirty. Will you come get me?"

Eddie the Nerd, the geek said uncomplicated, "Yes. And where are you?"

He arrived a half-hour later. Asked if she needed coffee before going home?

"No, just take me home," she replied, then threw up on his car's seat and herself.

The Nerd was gentle, and kind, and soft-spoken. He was understanding, and helpful, and knew just what Norma Jean needed. When they got to her mother's house, he helped her up the walk, worried if she would be able to make it to work. Asked if she needed a ride? Could he pick her up after work?

And, the next twenty times when she called him at that appalling hour he was still gentle, and kind, and soft-spoken, and understanding, and helpful and knew just what she needed. During those rides home, he would talk to her about his day, careful never to ask about what she was doing with herself. Up the walk he would walk her, taking care to hold the door for her, offering to drive her to work. For all his effort, she still refused to go out with "a Nerd."

And, so twenty-five more times she called him in the middle of the night and twenty-five more times he came to pick her up. And, gently, and kindly, and under-spoken, and understandingly, and helpful, he brought her home and deposited her safely in her house; No questions, no blame, no retribution. Not a hint of any of it. He only wished to help her, yet, at the same time satisfy his need to be near her. For him, her heart was in his heart and he increasingly wanted to be with her. Copiously, he called to ask for a date. Again, again and again he would call, but she wouldn't date the Nerd.

And, so it went for months; then a year had pasted. In February, Eddie bought her a gold necklace, for Valentine's

Day. Eddie, the nerd, bought her a bouquet of flowers for her April birthday. Then a precious gem for no reason at all.

"It's precious like you," He had said when he gave her a diamond necklace.

Each month he found something to buy her. Each month it brought a smile to her face. Suddenly, she realized that she looked forward to those thoughtful gifts. Twenty-five more times she called him in the middle of the night and twenty-five more times he picked her up to drive her home; no questions, and no blame, and no retribution.

Well into the second year of "the Nerd" and Norm Jean, he include a message, his first message he ever had written her. It was a defining moment of her life. The words were profound and caused her insides to tingle in some funny way she didn't really understand. He had written on the card that accompanied the dozen red roses.

"Wherever you go, my heart goes with you;
Whatever you do, I will do with you;
Whenever you call, I will come;
My heart is with your heart - Forever."

She sat down as she read the card. She read it over, and over, and over, again. Her beautifully, sensuous eyes narrowed and filled with tears. In her thirty-four years no one had ever said anything like this to her. For the longest time, she thought about the late hours she called the Nerd. All the times in the middle of night he came for her. He never once refused. She thought of his gentleness and kindness. How he was helpful and supportive. She thought about all the gifts he had given her, never asking anything in return. How he warmly talked with her girls when she occasionally did let him come into the house. She read the card once more then did something not anyone would have guessed. She made two phone calls, the first one to work and a second one to the Nerd.

"I need to be with you right now." She said quietly in his ear.

A few minutes later she heard his soft knock on the door.

* * * * *

Norma Jean sat in the office, thinking. What would she say to Eddie, her Nerd, and how would she say it? He has a big game coming in June. An important game he's been preparing for all year.

"I can't take this away from him," she thought.

It's his whole life, something he has been wanting for years. All he has talked about. She can't spoil it for him, not now, not ever.

The pain shot through her hip and down her leg. It caused her to sit straighten in the chair. She waited for it to pass. Norma Jean looked at the pain prescription and thought about what the doctor had said. Well, happy sixty-third birthday she thought. Happy Birthday! How would she tell her Nerd? She took hold of her sister's hand and squeezed gently.

"Take me for a drive," she said flatly. She stood up, put the prescription and referral in her purse. With purpose, she walked out to her sister's car. When Norma Jean's sister caught up, she asked, "What will you tell him?"

"Don't know," Norma Jean replied. "Just take me for a drive so I can think."

Out of town they drove. Toward the mountains, the beautiful mountains she enjoyed over the years of their married life. How many times had they come up here on a camping trip with the girls; or, at times, just the two of them? The peaceful woods, she thought. And, the rivers frothing and flowing by their camp site.

He would fish. She would sit in her beach chair drinking a beer, reading a book. Occasionally, she would look up at him. He'd be so proud when he reeled in a "nice one". When he had caught enough, he would clean them with care and fry them up. Later, together they would sit-by the evening fire, watching the flames dance, watch the glow dim as the fire faded, watching together the night take hold.

The time between when night settles-in and the sun drifts below the horizon, is a soft, magical time when the forest puts to sleep its day creatures and brings out its night dwellers. It is a time when the air gets thick with a chill and the clouds become redder from the sinking sun.

It was a time when he would hold her and they would talk; sometimes, they made love, gentle, tender love. They were soul-mates caring for each other.

Finally, evening would change into night, cold and clear. The air was fresh and contained a nip. Together, they would snuggle down in the camper, holding each other tight. "Good night, Love." He would whisper in her ear. She would squeeze his arm and then fall asleep with her head on her nerd's chest.

In the morning, she would wake to find him gone. He would be along the banks of the glistening river, casting a line, and then bring back his catch. Again, he would clean the fish with care and then fry them for breakfast. The wind would rustle the leaves and she could smell the coffee as the day would brighten and the day creatures returned to the land.

To the door of the camper, he came, knocking gently. A cup of coffee in-hand for her, fixed just the way she liked it. Norma Jean thought about all this as her sister drove high, and higher, and deeper into the mountains. She thought about his love for her and her love for him.

I didn't love him enough, not as much as he loved me. What about the mostly good times they had together? "What do I say," she thought out-loud almost forgetting her sister was there? Oh God! God, what have you done?

"Why don't you take a trip to Hawaii," Norma's sister said, interrupting Norma Jean's thoughts. She watched the road for falling rocks, or worse, yet, for a deer jumping out.

Norma Jean thought for a few moments, as though she needed time to pull herself back from the camping trips and the fishing expeditions.

"Hawaii?" she finally asked out loud. "Why, Hawaii?"

"You said you always wanted to go there," her sister answered. "Why not go now before it's too ... ?" Her voice trailed off and she couldn't decide if she had said the right thing. "Oh, Norma, I didn't mean to sound cold."

Norm Jean looked at her sister for a moment, remembering she always had a knack for saying something at the wrong time. Straight forward was the way her mother described Norma Jean's sister.

The forest went streaming by, the trees standing tall, reaching to the sky, while casting a canopy across the highway. Spring was bringing out the Queen Ann's Lace along the road and the yellow Mountain Daisies were beginning to bloom. She said aloud, "This will all be gone for me soon." She knew her sister meant well.

"It's OK." She stated, then firmly ordered, "Take me home."

She looked at her watch. It was getting late and Eddie would be coming home soon to fix dinner. It was Friday and he would be fixing pizza, getting ready to watch a movie he will have rented from the video store. Tomorrow night will be the kids, and friends, and spaghetti, or, since the weather is nice, probably a Bar-B-Q. She didn't know for sure and this time it really didn't matter. Just being with him would be enough. In fact, she really wanted to be with him, alone.

As they pulled into the slightly angled driveway, Eddie was just coming out of the camper. He was gray now. His hair thinner than when they first met but his beard was still neatly trimmed. His oval glasses were thicker. Norma Jean looked at him and thought he hasn't changed a bit, still my Nerd. My Nerd, I love, and love, and love. What do I say?

He came to the car door, stood for a moment looking at her with that gentle smile and those blues eyes that seem to say I know, know all about it. As she opened the door, he grabbed the door, swung it open. Being the gentleman he always has been, he helped her from the car.

When he had her out of the car, he took her into his arms and held her close. She reached her arms around him. She felt a tremor deep inside him. They held each other tightly. He whispered into her ear that they should go camping.

God, she thought, how does he do it, he always knows the right thing to say and do for me. How does he do it? Norma Jean leaned back in his arms and looked at his face for a moment. She placed her hand on his chest and could feel the beating of his heart and the tension of his muscles. "What do you know," she asked?

"I know that we need to talk," he replied quietly. "I know we need to be alone." He took her arms from around him and looked at her for a moment. "I know I'm scared."

He released her and turned, "Everything is packed and ready. I put your clothes in the camper closet. We are ready to go. We should have time to get to Windy Point before dark. While you setup the camper, I'll go catch dinner. Sound OK?"

"Great!" she said standing there, amazed. She thanked her sister, telling her she would call when they got back.

"What about the prescriptions?" Norma Jean sister asked.

"A couple more days won't matter?" Norma Jean answered.

Nonetheless, being the big sister she was, she asked for the prescriptions and said they would be waiting when Norma Jean got home.

As her sister was leaving, Norm Jean asked Eddie if they needed to get anything from the house. No, was the reply as he shut and locked the door.

"Bet he forgot something," she thought, but didn't question him anymore. She smiled. It was their little game whenever they were leaving on a camping trip.

After they got into the truck cab, he leaned across and kissed her on the cheek. She could see that his eyes were red and watery but he said nothing more. He started the truck. Once they were on the highway that would take them to their campground, he asked, "How bad is it for us?"

* * * * *

Friendships are a funny thing. They take many different forms and come in numerous combinations. Some friendships are work-based because two people work together, there they form a friendship. Others are based on location, where one lives, neighbors become friends because they live next to each other, or down the street and pass-by each other's house until one finally says come on in for a cup of coffee. Or, we're having a Bar-B-Q Saturday, stop by. Other friendships are based on common values and causes. One joins the PTA and meets others with school age children or husbands have a golf interest and the wives are thrown together and begin to bond with each other.

Norma Jean had one friend she called "The Blond." They had met at a softball game in which their husbands both played on the same team. Norm Jean would arrive at the game and sit up high in the bleachers, watching all the families and team members arrive.

A late arrival was The Blond. A perky little woman with a great big smile and she talked non-stop. The Blond held court with everyone, drank beer, cheered her husband on and didn't know anything about softball. She always sat about three rows below Norm Jean, talking with people in her row or below.

No one remembers for sure, although Norma Jean knows it was the third week of the season. The Blond arrived and happen to look up into the bleachers and saw Norma Jean. She waved and invited Norma to come down and sit with her. A friendship was born. It was one based on nothing more than they enjoyed the other's company. They spent the rest of the game drinking beer, laughing and talking. To this day they have no idea how the game turned out. The bond was formed and the friendship was destine to become tighter and tighter.

In the weeks, months and years, the friendship matured and each was telling the other their most intimate secrets. The Blond was married to man that was by outward appearances a good husband, but Norma Jean soon discovered he was a man that was selfish with his money, demanding of his wife and had little consideration for her feelings. Norma Jean, on the other hand, talked about her husband and told of his thoughtfulness and gentleness. How he had always been there for her and her two girls. The Blond listened and wished--she admired Norma's husband and thought what it must be like to have a husband like him.

And, so this friendship, started at a ball field, was based on the sharing of needs; a need for shopping, a need to laugh, a need to share stories and a need to share intimate secrets.

Norma Jean unconscientiously wanted to be more out-going and The Blond wanted a husband like Norma's. They became fast friends.

It was a haunting message left by Norma Jean. The Blond thought for a moment. She thought about the last ten years since her own husband had died and how their friendship had waned. Her new husband of nine years didn't seem to care for Norma Jean or the many Bar-B-Qs. The new husband didn't like softball and he wasn't a beer drinker. The friendship with Norma Jean faded with time and circumstance. It had been a long time since Norma's last call but this one sounded troubled. I'll call her tomorrow thought The Blonde. She never did.

One day a week or two later, The Blonde's husband was home when the phone range.

"Hello," he said loudly.

"Hi," A familiar voice from the past answered weakly. "Your wife around?"

"Norma Jean! No, no she's not. How are you?" He thought about all the Bar-B-Qs and dinners. How he missed going to them the last few years. It seemed family always came first, her family that is; the Blond's.

"Not good," replied Norma Jean in a meek voice. "When will she be home? I need to talk with her."

She began to cry, a soft sob that could be heard. "She was my best friend and I need her. Please tell her to call me. I need ... "

"Norma," he interrupted her. "What's wrong?"

"Cancer," she whispered. "I have it in my hip, my liver and my one lung." She paused a moment, caught her breath, then continued, "I'm going to beat it; I'm going to win. The chemo will works, and I know it will. If not, the doctor says I have a year at most. That's why I need her to call me. She's my best friend."

"I'm so sorry," he said quietly. "What can we do?"

"Have her call me," She answered, and then pleaded, "Pleaseee."

He heard the click as she hung-up the phone. He held his receiver for a moment before replacing it back on the console. He was numb. He wondered if his wife would understand how serious this situation. Norma Jean was a year younger than he was and it made him feel vulnerable.

My, God he thought to himself. He remembered from his MD-web page that cancer spread like hers is in its fourth stage. Less than ten percent of the people who have it survive more than six months. Chemo rarely works at this stage of the game. He pondered, "What to do? What can we do? For her, it's too late. Just her support I guess." This he was thinking as his wife came through the front door.

* * * * *

"How's your marriage," Norma Jean asked? The question caught the Blond off guard. She didn't answer right away. Looking over at Norma Jean, the Blond was thinking how frail she looked today. Her husband was right; Norma wasn't going to win, not against this sarcoma.

My marriage? How does she do it? How does she know the wrong questions to ask?

"Well, he lost my house, lost his job, has almost no income and can't get a job," she responded bitterly. "I'm going back to school to get my teaching credentials and will probably have to work until I'm seventy-five."

She hated the thought of going back to school. She felt old and would be un-welcomed by the younger people. Soon, she would be student teaching. The Blond just knew the students won't want this old lady teaching them. She would look ridiculous and just knew she would fail. All, because her husband had made bad choices and had done stupid things. She was embarrassed to tell anyone let alone Norma.

Staring morosely around the rented mobile home, she asked, "How would you like living in this tin can. The walls are all dark paneling and there is no light. I hate it. I feel like my life is out of control."

"'Betcha, he doesn't like it either," Norma replied.

"He doesn't care, Norma," she snapped back. Then she added, "He'd live in a piece of shit place and it wouldn't even bother him."

"It doesn't bother him to live here," she added looking around the hated mobile home with it miserable walls and dismal lighting, "The heating can't even keep up with the weather."

"This isn't a bad place," Norma Jean said. She looked around the living room, with it paneling of dark-oak and green rug. "You should've seen some of the places I've lived in," she added.

"Look around, it could be worse," she finally said, to console her friend, but could see it was not working. The Blond was in her own little world of feeling sorry for herself. Norma Jean knew not to say too much.

"I'm glad you came by today," she had said, changing the subject.

It had been a perfect day. The Blond had picked her up just before noon and they went to West Park for lunch. West Park was one of those little shopping malls with a locally owned market and several specialty shops and restaurants.

They ate at Quinn's Place and Norma had a bowl of beef bouillon. It was a leisurely lunch, in which two friends chatted, reconnecting those bonds which transform into a magic place called true friendship. They talked about the times they had spent together, when they worked together, when they had gone shopping together, when they had taken a trip together.

After visiting The Blond's home, they stopped for a Venti Green tea at Starbuck's. Excitedly, they recounted their trip together to Canada, to Vancouver B.C. But Time was closing in. They could feel its power, sense presence. Their time together was ending. The Blond dropped off her friend at the edge of Norma's slightly angled driveway.

When The Blond got home, her husband asked where she had been. She replied she had some free-time and decided to go see Norma.

She talked about what a great time they had together. How she had taken Norma to lunch. How they remembered their times together. How she had brought her to the house.

She said Norma liked the house. "But I know that she was just being kind," the Blond said with resignation. "How could anyone like this place?" The Blonde's husband said nothing, but thought, "I'm doing the best I can."

"Norma is very upbeat and knows that the chemo is working. She's lost a lot of weight," the Blond rattled on, continuing, "School will be starting next week and I'll be busy. But during my Christmas break we'll get together then."

The Blonde's husband looked at her and quietly said, "Norma will be gone by then. She won't make Christmas."

She looked at her husband, not saying anything, absorbed in how she would be busy with school and getting her credentials for teaching. Besides, Norma would understand, she thought.

* * * * *

The call came on a Saturday morning while the Blonde was attending her class. That was the second weekend in December. Norma Jean's youngest daughter was to the point, Without expression, and saying simply, "Tell your wife that Norma died Friday night. The funeral will be Wednesday at eleven."

The next day, an obituary read that Norma Jean had died peacefully at home surrounded by her loving family. It ended with the address of where the funeral service would be performed.

The white church sat just off the highway, tucked in to the depression of a hill. The tall, simple steeple pointed to heaven. When one looked at it, one could feel the calling of Middle American. This christen architect is, and has been, in thousands of cities and villages across the American landscape. The Mormons have always built a simple but eloquent stake, a church if you will. Patriotic people have worshiped in these stakes ever since their prophet found the foundations of the church in upstate New York.

Mormonism is distinctively an American institution and, because of this, it has been woven into the fiber of America history. It is here, at this local stake, that the friends of Norm Jean gathered that one gray morning to remember her, to talk about her, to help each other cope, to help each other with loss. Each knew something in their life had changed, and would never change back. Each knew that someone of value was gone. Some remembered a friendship; some remembered a mother and wife. One remembered that they should have been a better friend.

The Blond cried genuine tears and babbled to her husband about not being a good friend. That she should've taken more time to be with Norma during her last days. She had meant to visit again, but she had just been too busy.

"What was I supposed to do?" she cried. Guilt gripped her. She just knew that Norma's family was asking why she hadn't spent more time with their mother. But, I was busy, she thought silently. I had work and school and this time of the year, shopping. What was I to do; I had things to get done. She looked around her, all the people were sitting quietly. Leaning over to her husband, she said in a whisper, "I wasn't a very good friend, was I?"

He put his mouth up to her ear and said quietly, "Norma understood." Then added, "She was proud of the fact you are getting your teaching credentials."

Then he kissed her ear and patted her knee. How could he tell her change waits for no one? It is cold and merciless, and this is the secret of the Universe; change takes place constantly without favor and without feelings. It is relentless and never hesitates for anything or anyone.

* * * * *

The ashes of Norma Jean were placed at the foot of a beautiful gray Birch tree. In winter, one could appreciate its smoke colored bark with its deep rivulets spiraling up the trunk to the main limbs. The smaller branches look like gnarled twigs. In the spring, they will become covered with green, serrated leafs, called cut-leafs. Red veins will run through the leaves.

Black and white Mocking Birds, red-breasted Robins and yellow Finches will come to rest in the tree, to feed and to mate. Maybe some doves will appear. And, another season will lord over the land, spreading out over it, making everything right again.

And, Norm Jean will sleep peacefully, her heart carried in the hearts of those who loved her.

Mud Lake

It sits in the high country. Up high in the ancient forest of the Cascade Range. It's where spotted owls nest and marmots roam freely, poking their heads up and sitting on their haunches like targets in a shooting gallery. Travelers on Highway 12 whiz drive-by; some take aim.

The Whitetail deer, along with the stealthy cougar, come to Mud Lake, each tolerating the other. The deer being safe until it's the cougar's feeding time.

The first time I heard of Mud Lake was from my friend, George. He suggested we (meaning myself, himself, and our mutual attorney friend Freddie) take some time off and go fishing together.

George, Freddie and I all graduated from the same university fifteen years ago and have since worked every moment of our fecund lives building successful careers. Freddie finished law school and we all moved to the Northwest, met our future wives, had babies and made our lives moderately victorious.

When George suggested a fishing trip, Freddie carped, "We just came back from vacation." He was right. Our three families recently come back from a demanding, nerve-racking trip to Disneyland with the wives and kids. Getting back to work felt more like the vacation.

"No," George explained to Freddie and me, "just us three." He waited a moment before continuing. "It would be like a guys' vacation. Just us men," he described emphatically. "Maybe, camping, or something like that."

Freddie and I looked each another, then, said in unison, "Great idea!" . . . "But to where?" we asked.

That's when George said, "Mud Lake, of course, camping!"

I knew nothing about camping, and even less about Mud Lake. But George said he knew. That he would coach us and he said we would enjoy camping and fishing—just for a week. It would be our chance to get in touch with our primitive male sides, plus a break from the wives and kids. Oh, yes, after a week at Disneyland, Freddie and I were both ready.

As Marcus Aurelius once said, "The die is cast." And so it was. Mud Lake was now on our radar and we were pumped full throttle. Two weeks later we left.

* * * * *

Mud Lake isn't overly large and has little or no tolerable beaches for humans to sunbath on. The deer have to stretch their necks through foliage and tree limbs to reach the cooling lake water. The vegetation grows so thick at the lake's edge, it's almost impossible to launch a canoe. Even an air raft would be difficult to get through the shoreline's thicket.

Prehistoric Sequoias have guarded the lake for eons, since before the Christian era. Larkspurs, pines, and cypress have combined over the ages, along with a multitude of various ferns, to block the way for anyone wanting to introduce into this pristine woodland something as outlandish as a damn canoe.

Only inept and unskilled campers, like us three, would even dare to stay at the lake, let alone fish it. Nevertheless, we three crude and incompetent fishermen made our way through the under-growth, tattered plant parts, teeming fauna and flora, all better known as the duff to engage our manhood.

To Mud Lake and its surrounding forest floor came us, three naïve and unproven campers, professional men, men of letters and occupations—one a skilled craftsman, the other a lawyer, and the third a techno geek. All of us have received our college degrees from the university, and we are successful in our chosen fields. We longed for a macho experience, sometime off of work, and time away from our wives and our high-spirited kids. Now we were getting it. For each of us, it was the first attempt at communing with the great outdoors. What more could a real man want?

None of us really had a grasp of the outdoor experience; because of this, like most people learning something new, we were a bit uncomfortable in our new roles as outdoorsmen. That being said, we were resolved to partake in this new and exciting experience, anticipating that progress involves some discomfort, but we brought enough beer to bolster up any doubts about our courage or inabilities.

Before launching this trip, we spent plenty of hours and plenty of money in the local Cabela's. And, we had an in-store camping/fishing expert who suggested exactly what was needed to have a successful week in the highlands of the old growth forest. Also, the saleslady assured us of an experience we would never forget. And, as it turned out, she was right! Our first obstacle; that was, after figuring out how to pack everything so it could be carried into the backcountry, was just locating the damn lake. Since I was the technical guru, I of course whipped out my portable GPS system from my pocket and proceeded to tell us the way. "It's just four hours to the north." I pontificated pointing at what I thought was true north.

After getting an early start at 5 a.m., we finally found the lake fourteen hours later. We discovered afterwards we had only hiked by it twice that day. By this time, the sun was towards the west, sinking into the Pacific for the night. It was still very hot, but we figured for amateurs, we're doing great.

"Hey look, a lake!" George had bellowed, pushing aside some bushes as the rest of us blindly walked by. He then suggested that we circumvent the lake; that on the opposite side was a small beach. It sounded good to Freddie and me.

When we arrived at the tiny beach, we were all bushed from the "five" mile hike from the road to the lake. George immediately extracted a six pack of beer from the canoe, in which we had hauled all our gear. He tied a line to the cans, and then he threw them in the lake with a hearty heave. His thinking was a cold lake will chill the beer while we set up camp.

It wasn't until we were all sweaty and hot from setting up the camp that we discovered he hadn't tied the knot correctly to the six-pack. When Freddie pulled the line in, there was no beer attached.

Freddie yelled at George, rebuking him that he hadn't connected the line to the beer correctly. Freddie questioned George as to what to do.

George simply walked out to where he thought the beer lay, took a deep breath, and drove under the water. He came up a couple minutes later all wet and covered with mud, bitching that the six-pack was there but something lay across it.

Taking another deep breath, he dove back under the water and re-appeared with the six-pack in his hand. He proudly displayed it by holding it over his head. "BEER!" he yelled, as a couple of squirrels darted off.

As we gathered lakeside, George gave us each a beer. "A nice cold one, at long last," he said. We sat on a large tree limb and took in the beauty of the evening as the setting sun was nearing the top of the mountains to the west.

Once camp was setup, we were ready to cook the evening meal and enjoy the refreshing cold beer.

"This is it fellows," I crowed. "This is great, us three and nature."

As my two friends agreed, none of us noticed the configuration that had surfaced just a few feet off shore, at about the spot where George had recovered the beer.

"Let's get dinner started," I bellowed. "I could eat a horse!"

Freddie yelled he would cook, George said he would throw more beer in the lake to cool, and I broke out the spam and canned beans for Freddie to cook. As he got ready to cook the evening meal, he called out to George, "George, tie that beer securely." The smell of the evening meal curled-up and drifted from the finely built fire Freddie had put together.

The evening breeze had tested his outdoors skills but in the end he conquered the task. It was a nice fire, which allowed him to warm the pork 'n beans and the spam. We each were dished good size servings of dinner and when finished, we were replete. Another beer would top off the long day and evening and I could hardly wait to slip into my new tent.

It was about nine-thirty, sunset had long passed, and Freddie was strumming his banjo in the dusk of the evening. We were beginning to settle in for the night when George decided one more beer was needed.

"C'mon guys," he taunted us, "one more beer, then, to sleep."

"Not me," I said. "I'm dead tired." Freddie nodded agreement and dove into his tent. "Enough fun for one day. I'm going to bed," he called out as he dropped the flap on his tent.

The last thing I saw as I entered my tent was George heading down to the lake to get himself a beer. I was exhausted and was sure I would be asleep before my head hit the pillow of my two hundred dollar sleeping bag. Yes, a bit of overkill, but the Cabela's saleswoman assured me it would prevent snakes from sharing a warm bed with me. "Gotta watch out for those rattlers," she had assured me in her best outdoor professional pitch. How was I to know there were no rattlers at this altitude? Against the peaceful evening, and waking me out of a dead sleep, came a cry of unbelievable intensity.

The fear in the cry was strong and abounding, echoing off the lake and through the trees. If there were deer, or cougars about, no doubt after George's blood-cuddling cry they would have headed for the furthest meadow.

As I swiftly came out of my tent, I saw a raccoon dart into a thicket of ferns behind Freddie's tent. Up from the lake, moving with speed I never knew he had, came George.

"Oh, shit," he yelled. "Oh, shit!" He ran to us, jumping up and down, pointing towards the lake. He looked at me and yelled, "You won't believe it!" Then to Freddie, who had just cleared his tent, he yelled again, "Neither will you."

I took one look at George and said, "George, calm down. We can't understand you."

George was literally shaking in his new hiking boots. He pointed to the lake several times and tried to form words, but nothing coherent came out.

Again, I tried to calm him, but he took off towards the lake saying, "Follow me." He took a few more hurried steps, looked to the lake then back to Freddie and I, saying, "Hurry-up, Damn it, hurry."

When we finally caught up with him at the edge of the lake, he was again pointing towards where the beer had been chilling. "Look," he said. "Look! Look, Freddie, look!"

"Look at what? Freddie asked as he peered out on the moonlit lake. Then, Freddie turned to George, and said, "What'cha you do, lose the damn beer? Did you throw the six-pack out again without tying it correctly?"

"No, Freddie," George stammered. "Look right there," he said pointing. "Don't you guys see it?"

I had my new all-weather, seventy-five dollar flashlight hanging at my side. Once again, the Cabela's saleslady said it was a must for anyone bent on spending the night in the mountains. I whipped it out with blazing speed, like a true outdoorsman, and focused it to where George had been pointing.

At first, I didn't see anything. Then George grabbed my arm and swung the light further to the right. Something was floating in the water.

It was big, bloated, and bluish. Oh God, it was a human body! "Jesus," I shouted and ran down the shoreline towards the massive thing to get a better look.

I stood there aiming my flashlight at the bilious mass, noting by the exposed chest that "the thing" was probably a woman. I felt Freddie come up behind me, while down the beach George was vomiting.

"What the hell is it?" Freddie asked, more amazed than curious. He couldn't take his eyes off the distended physique. Hideous, repulsive, and gruesome would all be adequate descriptors.

"A body," I answered, than added, "A dead body."

"A dead body?" Freddie asked, revolted and shocked.

I nodded and said simply, "Looks to be female."

George rejoined us, standing together on the beach looking at the chilling and unsightly intrusion. We were the three manly men being fearless, we, the macho men doing the outdoor experience. We, three best friends doing a guy's vacation together. The Cabela's saleswoman was right, again, when she said it would be a vacation we would never forget.

For what seemed like eons of time, we stood there staring at the body as it bobbed just below the surface. I felt like we were at a wake, only this person was a total stranger. What had happened to the person we didn't know. My curiosity got the better of me and I started wading into the water to get a closer look.

Freddie, realizing what I was doing, shouted, "What the hell are you doing? He ran over to me and as he grabbed my arm, said, "Stop this! You can't go in there."

"Why not?" I asked. Being the lawyer, he began explained to me all the legal reasons why I shouldn't touch or get near the body.

I replied, "Freddie, you sound like a lawyer." I continued to wade out to the body. "I am a lawyer, dummy," he called out to me.

As I approached the corpse, I shined my light on what appeared to be her head. Dead-center, just above the bridge of the nose was a large hole, the burnt skin around the cavity made me conclude it was a bullet hole.

"Good god, Freddie," I called to my friend, "it's murder." I ran my light beam over the rest of the body, linger at the chest, then scanned the rest down to the toes that floated just above the surface. Everything was so swollen, and I was so inexperienced, I couldn't detect if anything else was amiss.

Freddie, still standing on the beach, asked, "How do you know?"

"There's a big hole in the forehead," I answered. "Between the eyes." I felt someone rush out into the water behind me then stop just at my back. It was George. I couldn't see his face in the dark but I could tell it was him by his breathing.

"Show me," he commanded. I returned my flashlight to the head and then heard a rustle of water as George hurriedly backed up to the beach and heaved again. "Now that's manly," I thought to myself.

Turning back to shore, I flashed my light on Freddie who was still trying to view the body in the dark. I waded carefully away from the body and back up to where Freddie was standing.

I turned off the light as Freddie asked, "What do we do now?" "You're the lawyer," I shot back. Standing there in the dark, I felt totally helpless. I heard Freddie give a low sigh, he was frustrated.

"We need to report this immediately," he finally said. I could barely make out his silhouette as he headed back toward the campfire. "We need to report this," he repeated.

I followed him back to our camp where we found George weak and wan. I asked him if he was feeling better but he just kind of groaned at me.

Minutes later he said, "God, I've never seen anything so hideous. It's revolting." He sat there, a beer in one hand, the other rubbing his prodigious stomach. "God, what do we do now?" he repulsively asked.

"Report this, that's what," Freddie said as he took a chair next to George. He grabbed a beer from George's six-pack, snapped it open and took a long draw, then he pulled out his cell phone.

In the dark, it made his face glow and I could see his eyes searching for any signs of a connection. "No bars," he concluded, taking a quick gulp of beer. "We're too high up."

I sat down on a log that was next to the fire and reach for a beer. "Then we can't report it tonight. There's no cell service up this high, and we can't hike down to the car because it's dark. Besides, it would be dangerous."

Freddie and George looked at me, then at each other and nodded to one another.

Slowly George asked, "Are we just going to stay up here?"

"Seems to be the only thing we can do, at this point," I answered him, adding, "I'm not risking hiking in the dark. One could get lost, run into an animal, or fall into a ravine."

Freddie agreed, but seemed uncomfortable with the decision. "We need to report this," he said again.

George hadn't said much up to this point, but now he squirmed in his chair. "I don't know what to do," he puzzled. "And, what pisses me off is it's our first ever vacation since we moved up here."

He thought for a moment, then, said, "What the hell difference would it make if we didn't report the thing until the end of the week, when we go back to the car?"

Freddie the lawyer was quick to respond, "We can't do that, man, it ain't right. Besides, it will make us accessories after the fact. I'd lose my license." He thought for a moment, then concluded, "Besides the victim deserves better than that."

George belched a loud beer burp, then, said weirdly, "Hell, we deserve better than this. Who'll know when we found her? Damn it, we could say we didn't see the body until Friday night. Who'll know?"

I looked at George as he sat in his lawn chair, the campfire reflecting his features made him look like he was acting, grotesque. In all the time I've known George never has he acted bizarre, that is, until tonight. People act a bit wacky when confronted with death. It's not something they deal with on a daily basis; perhaps being whacky is to be expected.

"George," Freddie finally said, "I'm not happy with that. I know we can't go tonight, but we do need to go down tomorrow morning, find a signal, and call it in."

"Yeah, well good luck," George replied absently. He looked at Freddie vaguely for a moment, then, pulled the tab off another beer.

I could sense the antagonism building. "Look, we don't need to make a decision right now," I cheerily injected. "Let's talk about it in the morning. We all need to get some sleep."

Both Freddie and George looked at me with astonishment. "How can we sleep?" George asked as he took a long pull on his beer. "Maybe you can, but I can't," he claimed. "I'm staying up. God knows, that killer may still be lurking around."

"And if he is?" I asked George, "What are you going to do about it?

"I'll kick his ass!" George bellowed back at me. "I'll take his gun and shove it up his ass, that's what!"

Freddie looked at me. We both laughed at the same time.

"George, get some sleep," I bellowed back at him jauntily. "We'll talk about it in the morning." With that, I went into my tent and crawled into my posh sleeping bag.

* * * * *

That was a long, long night that night. A dead body nearby is not something conducive to sleep. I could hear Freddie and George still talking. George was lamenting the fact the body had ruined our vacation while Freddie was still determined we must do the right thing.

"Going down the mountain in the morning is the right thing to do, George," Freddie was saying.

I heard another beer can open, guessed it was George, and heard him ask, "Who the hell puts a bullet in someone's head?"

Minutes passed before I heard Freddie's reply, "I don't know. I remember this one case I read about. The guy had cut his wife's throat. Then, he decided it wasn't enough and in a rage he disemboweled her. God, the crime scene photos were horrifying, just nasty."

"What the hell kind of guy does that?" George asked.

"I don't know," Freddie answered, then, added, "the guy was a brilliant artist, plus he was a well-respected teacher. His students loved him, the faculty all loved him, and his three kids loved him. He was passionate about his work and it showed. He had quite a name in the art world."

I found myself listening through my tent carefully as George reflected quietly, "Freddie, men have the capacity to create beautiful things. Those same men also can do atrocious things to others, sometimes even to their own loved ones."

"I know," answered Freddie dubiously. "I don't get it, but that's how it has been throughout history. Men create beautiful art, great music, unbelievable architecture, and incredible inventions, yet, they can just as easily destroy each other. Why? I don't know, never been able to fathom the reasons. It's a fatal flaw of some sort."

They were quiet for a few minutes. I could hear George drinking his beer. Freddie must have lit his pipe because I could smell the sweet cherry blend tobacco aroma waif its way into my tent.

Somewhere out on the lake, I heard a fish jump out of the water in pursuit of a beasty insect that had landed in the surface.

"It has to do with the sex-drive," George pondered, picking up the thread of the conversation. "It's built into our DNA. It's all about power."

I heard Freddie give a laugh, "What are you saying, George? You're nuts."

"No, I'm not," a serious George replied, "Think about those rape cases you've defended. It wasn't about sex for those men. It was about power, domination. They wanted to dominate the woman. That's what they got off on. That's the fatal flaw."

Freddie was on George like a wolf on a rabbit in the dead of winter. "You're telling me that men commit terrible atrocities because of their sex-drive?" There was a pause, then I heard Freddie add, "C'mon George, you've had too much beer. It's time for bed."

George let go with another beer burp, then, answered, "I'm telling you, it's tied to our sex-drive, along with our egos. Wars, killing, great art, building great things, it's all about domination and power. Think about it, wars are fought for domination, killing is for control. Great businesses are built out of the need for power which, of course, we call greed. But in the end it all comes down to pro-creation. I don't care what anybody says, it comes from our need to fuck." With that, I heard George throw his beer can in the trash box and walk off.

"Going to bed, Freddie," George disgustedly announced. "See you in the morning."

A few minutes passed before I heard Freddie sigh and give his pipe a few raps on a rock. Then Freddie gave out a, "Wow!" followed by "Good night, George."

* * * * *

In mornings there is a wonderful time between the first light of dawn and actual sunrise. It is a quiet time, a time when the forest is awaking. Birds begin to call out, announcing the end of darkness and the beginning of the daily foraging. Chicks in the nest are stretching their necks, demanding that first meal of the day while the parents scout out a fat insect.

A fawn in the undergrowth stirs, its camouflaged spots moving ever so slightly as a morning chill riffles through the tiny creature's back. She pulls her covered eyes from beneath her foreleg and looks into the dense stand of ferns for mother.

Mother, a few feet away, is quietly taking in the morning, her nose in the air checking for danger. Sounds cause her ears to twitch and turn, evaluating each jangle for its safety. When she is comfortable with her appraisal she will rise slowly, checking her surroundings over and over for potential danger. When she feels secure and safe, she will go indirectly to her young for the morning feeding.

Along the shoreline of Mud Lake a human form stirs, then crawls out the tent shelter. George stands up, stretches, and farts. He sleepily goes to edge of the lake and begins to relieve himself. Suddenly he is aware of his surroundings and, that, of the floating corpse just offshore from where he is pissing.

He looks out at the body as two black crows take flight. One of the crows has something in its beak, which George has to squint to see it in the early morning light.

"Oh, shit," He yells out! "Freddie! Freddie! Thomas! You guys gotta see this. It's sick." He keeps yelling for us to "Come see."

As we arrive, George is pointing to the crow on the left, yelling, "See it? See it."

"See what?" Freddie yells back as he struggles to see the crow. Then, suddenly it registers and he confirms, "Oh, my God, it's an eye!"

As I draw-up next to George, he answers with, "Damn straight! That fucking crow pulled out her eye." He's at the edge of the lake, gawking at the body. "Yep, one eye is gone. Jesus!"

Freddie just stands there, stunned. Finally, he says, "Amazing." He turns back to the camp, leaving poor George there in utter disbelief. "I'm going to make breakfast," he calls back.

I follow Freddie back to camp. Having seen the sight of that poor woman has left me with no appetite. "Freddie, how can you eat?" I ask.

"Easy, I'm hungry," Freddie replies, and grabs a frying pan. In a few minutes the smell of bacon filled the air. I could imagine the bobcats and bears gathering back in the trees.

* * * * * *

East of White Pass ski resort, the white heavy cruiser glided along Highway 12, smoothly, just below the speed limit. The engine of the Crown Victoria hummed with the even-sound of a high performance engine waiting to be unleashed. It had the ability to accelerate from zero to sixty in less than eight seconds but was heavy enough to hold the curves of the road. The Washington State Patrol had chosen the perfect vehicle for the highways and freeways of the nation's 42nd state. On each side of the cruiser is embossed, "State Patrol" over a lightning bolt.

Officer Frank Tuttle is driving.

Frank Tuttle met the physical standards of the Patrol, he's over six feet tall, buff, and he's well educated, having a degree in criminal justice, which gives him an advantage over his fellow officers. He's passed a battery of psychological tests. In fact, he scored extremely well on all the tests.

His three tours of duty to the Middle East had left him in sound condition, even with two major battles that saw several of his fellow marines killed or maimed. As he liked to say, he holds no grudges, but "give me a black turban at 200 yards and I'll give you a guy with a hole in his head."

This morning, Frank was cruising the highway at a modest speed. His pre-trip for duty showed nothing out of the ordinary. He was enjoying the smooth ride and the early morning beauty and quiet. Calls coming across the radio were low-keyed: an abandoned vehicle along the road down by Gold Creek; a traffic stop over by Dog Lake; and, another call about a lost puppy in Woodinville. It's one of the very reasons that Frank loved duty in the mountains. The down-time is about ninety-eight percent of the time, with the rest being pure adrenaline rush. Something he needed from time to time.

As he was cruising along, he heard his number called to meet a detective unit of the patrol at Trail Head 72. "Proceed, Code 1," the female radio voice crackled. "10-4," Frank responded.

He eased his cruiser to the side of the road to start his U-turn back to the Mud Lake trail head, a small parking zone seldom used by hikers. Nobody in their right mind hikes to Mud Lake, he thinks. He'd been there once, and once was enough.

* * * * *

Morning breakfast was over by six. Freddie had eaten his weight in bacon, eggs and beans. I had finally succumbed to the aroma of the bacon and ate a bit. The thought of the dead woman still made me sick, but I also knew that we would be heading down the mountain soon, and I needed my protein. George, well, George just had a couple of beers. In each beer, he'd put a raw egg and tomato juice, then, guzzled them down.

"George, you better lighten up on the beer," Freddie advised him. "It's a five mile hike down the mountain. Sure you don't want some food?"

"Fuck no!" George responded. Ole' George was in one of his moods, the kind when we like not to be around him. "I still don't see why we can't wait to Friday," he probed Freddie. "She ain't going any place."

Freddie looked at his friend dubiously. "George, didn't you hear anything I said last night," he barked at his mollycoddled friend? "It would make us accessories after the fact, George. Is that what you want, to be an accessory?"

"Naw, I guess not," a dejected George answered. "I just wanted to have some extra time together."

"Hey, we can come back, my friend," Freddie replied. "We'll have the rest of the week, George. But right now we have to do the right thing, the legal thing."

"Ok, Ok," George replied as he stuck a few beers in his back pack and nothing else.

"George, you acting weird," I said to him. I watched him put in two more beers. "You better include some spam and crackers," I advised him. He seemed to hate even the thought of going down the mountain.

He looked over at the floating body, again, then he turned to us, saying, "Maybe I should stay here with her. Ya know, to keep the damn crows off her.

Freddie and I looked at each other. Freddie said, "That's not a good idea George. We need to say together, as a group, so that we can be witnesses for each other. Otherwise, under the laws we could get accused of wrongdoings."

"How's that Freddie?" I asked. "Good God, she was dead for days before we found her."

"You don't know that," Freddie countered. "The water in the lake is ice cold. There's no tellin how long she been here." He paused a moment, then, re-asserted, "No, we all need to go as a group. George, she'll be fine, believe me."

"Ok," George replied, "If that's your best legal advice?"

"It is!" Freddie assured George.

George muttered something under his breath, chugged the beer he was holding and then threw the can in the can box. "Let's go get this done," he belched out. The three of us pickup our backpacks, flung them onto our backs, and headed down the mountain.

About halfway down, Freddie pulled out his cell phone and stated excitedly that two bars were available. He dialed 911 and began reporting what we had discovered up at the lake. After answering a few questions, he put the phone away and said, "A state patrol car will meet us at the bottom." He seemed relieved.

The three of us continued down the mountain stopping only once, for George to pee. It was a beautiful Northwest day and I too found myself regretting having to leave the lake.

* * * * *

As the trail began to level out, we could see down to the trail head. A tall, uniformed officer was stand at the entrance to the trail with his hands on his belt buckle. As we came out from the trail, he tipped his hat to us and pointed towards his state patrol car.

"Good morning, gentlemen," He greeted us in a friendly, but professional tone. "Please step over to the car. Are you the gentlemen that called about the body?"

Freddie immediately stepped towards the officer, extended his hand quickly. It was a quick move and the officer reacted with a step backward, pointed to the car, and ordered, "Step to the car, NOW!"

Caught off-guard, Freddie pulled his hand down and stepped quickly towards the car. He looked at the officer's name tag and said, "Officer Tuttle, my name is Freddie Thompson. I'm a lawyer from Yakima."

George and I had already gone to stand by the car. As Freddie came up to us, he gave George and me a look that meant he would do the talking. "These are my friends George Ballard and Tom Grady," he said, pointing to each of us respectfully.

With that, George and I started to remove our backpacks but Officer Tuttle stopped us immediately.

"Do not remove your backpacks!" he commanded. Then he asked us, "Are any of you carrying any weapons, such as guns, knives, or blades of any type?" He asked, still with his thumbs looped to his belt. He watched us closely as we each shook our heads no, then, looking at each other, we each answered, "No."

"Do you mind if I get a beer out of my pack?" George suddenly asked. "It's hot, and I'm thirsty," he added, almost childlike.

The officer looked at him and indicated for George to step forward. George stood in front of the office, almost military like. Tuttle asked him what was in the backpack and was visually checking George out.

"Step to the front of the car," the officer ordered him. He looked at Freddie and I, "You gentlemen stay-put. Don't open your backpacks and keep your hands where I can see them." He then went to the front of the car with George, all the while never turning his back on any of us. You could tell he was well-trained and had experience at doing this. George was ordered to empty everything out of his pockets. He did, setting all his pocket contents on the hood of the patrol car. Then the officer patted him down and said to take off his backpack and open it. The trooper glanced at Freddie and me several times while he worked with George. We were both careful to stay in view and stand quietly. We didn't dare speak, either.

As George held open his backpack for the patrolman to look, a black, unmarked car drove into the small parking area. Freddie pointed at it, saying under his breath, "State Patrol detectives. See the plates?"

I looked at the plates, which had the familiar "WSP" letters followed by three numbers. As the car slowly passed us, in the back window I could also detect a slim, low-riding light bar. The car's tires were black, the wheels were plain, and the entire vehicle had the look of a typical undercover car.

Two tall plain clothed detectives got out of the car and walked towards us. They were both looking at a clipboard. The blond-hair fellow with wraparound sunglasses called-out, "I'm Detective Smith, which of you is Freddie Thompson?" Freddie held up his hand.

He directed Freddie to the other side of their car, out of ear shot and proceeded to have a lengthy conversation with him. George had returned to stand beside me. I couldn't hear what was being said, but I could tell it was bothering George. He was jittery.

"Damn," he said aloud. "I sure could use a beer."

The other detective, who was now standing with us, told George it might be better to wait. "Smith will want to talk with you in a few," he said in a friendly tone.

About ten minutes later, Freddie returned with Detective Smith following him. Freddie gave me and George a funny look, then, mouthed the words, "We got a problem."

Just as he finished uttering those words, the dark-hair detective pointed at me and said to accompany him to their car. I followed his instructions, and we stood by the black car, out of earshot of both my friends.

The detective asked me my full name and for my driver's license, which I quickly produced from my hip pocket. I then asked, "Is there some problem, Officer?"

The officer was examining my license closely, then, wrote some information on his clip board. Looking up at me, he asked, "Some problem? There's a dead body up there." As he pointed up towards the lake, he asked, "Is everything current on your license?"

"Yes," I answered. How stupid of me, I thought.

"Mr. Grady," the detective asked, "Can you, account for your time last Thursday afternoon? Say from about 1:00 p.m. to 5:00 p.m.?"

The question caught me totally off-guard. I had to really think about it. Good god, where was I that day? I start to rebuild my recollection of that day by remembering the three of us left for our camping trip the following Saturday morning. I remembered we left for our trip at about five in the morning on Saturday.

Friday night, after I was through packing for the trip, I took the wife and kids to the local Red Robin for burgers, got home about 7:30, watched Jeopardy, then, went to bed. I related this all to the officer.

"I'm asking about Thursday," he replied coldly, "not Friday."

"Oh, yes, Thursday," I thought out loud. "Let, see." I paused a moment while I reconstructed Thursday in my mind. I remembered I worked in the morning, went to lunch at Appleby's with some friends. Then, suddenly, I busted out with, "We went to Cabala's. I needed to get some different lures, Freddie met me there." I looked at the officer, then, added, "I think we were there for two or three hours."

"Go any place after that?" the detective probed me.

"Think I went home after that," I thought a moment, then, said, "No, wait. I stopped off at Petco to pick up some dog food." The detective just stared at me. I got nervous, then, added, "Dog food. You know. To make sure there was enough for the week. While I was gone." He continued to stare at me. I added more, "Ya know, while I was camping. I didn't want the wife any madder at me."

As the detective was writing notes on our conversation, I noted that a park ranger was coming down out from the trailhead that led to the lake. He motioned for Detective Smith to join him and they had a private conversation with the ranger pointing up towards the lake.

After about ten minutes I heard the blonde detective say he would call it in. Then he headed for his car, leaned in through the driver's window grabbed the radio microphone and began to talk.

In the meantime, the detective that was interviewing me said I could rejoin my friends, but warned me not to talk about the interview.

When I got back to Freddie and George, both were hot and sweaty. George nervously cracked open another beer, then, asked, "What the fuck did he ask you?"

I looked at Freddie, who seemed just fine, then, I studied George, then answered, "Just the usual stuff, my name and address."

"What else?" George pushed. "What else did he want to know?"

"George, calm down," I looked at George, realizing this whole thing was really upsetting him. "Hey, they are just asking normal questions." I looked at Freddie and asked him to help George compose himself.

Freddie hesitated a moment, then very professionally asked George, "George, do you need legal representation?"

George looked stunned by the question. I was stunned. George took another swig of his newly opened beer and answered, "Why the hell would I need a fucking lawyer? Jesus, Freddie, have you gone mad?" George acted offended by the question.

Freddie waited a moment, then, countered with, "Well, you seem upset and are acting like you have something to hide."

Before George could answer, Officer Tuttle came over and told George the two detectives would like a word with him over at their car. "You two are to remain here with me," he commanded.

George look at Freddie and me, started to say something to Freddie but then abruptly turned and went over to the detectives. The two detectives focused their attention on him and it looked like they asked him to empty his pockets.

Big officer Tuttle stayed with us, asking a few seemingly harmless questions. He asked whose car did we come up in, what time did we leave Saturday morning, who found the lake since it was our first time up here, and, finally, who first discovered the body. Freddie and I answered all his questions, but, then, the burly officer asked if George had been with us the whole time.

"Yes, of course," we answered the officer. "In fact, George was the one who wanted this trip so much," Freddie said, then looked at me and asked, "Isn't that true, Tom?"

I confirmed Freddie's information, then, added, "George has been pretty much with us every day this week." I looked at the officer and asked him, "What's going on? Are we under suspicion?

In his friendly but professional manner, he said, "No, no, just asking questions. Don't get the wrong idea. We're just trying to firm-up all the details."

It was precisely at this moment that I saw George turn toward us and call out for Freddie. "Freddie, get your ass over here," he yelled.

Freddie looked to Officer Tuttle questioningly and asked, "OK?" When the officer nodded in reply, Freddie walked quickly over to the detective's car and I heard him ask, "What's going on, George?"

As Freddie walked up to the detectives and George, he had asked George what was happening. George answered, "I need a lawyer." He paused a moment, then, added, "Least, I think I do."

Freddie looked at the two detectives, then, asked the one named Smith what was going on? To his dismay, the detective answered that they were considering arresting George on suspicion of murder.

"Who'd he supposedly murder?" Freddie quizzed the detective.

The second detective's answer baffled Freddie. The detective said, "We believe George knows more about the body in the lake, more than you might think."

"How can that be?" Freddie questioned. "We've been together most of this week and since Saturday morning constantly in each other's sight."

"Really?" questioned the blond detective. "Was George with you on Thursday?" He looked at George, then at Freddie apparently trying to read their body language. If he discerned anything, he didn't let on.

"Thursday? What'd we do on Thursday?" He thought for a full five minutes. It must have been a madding five minutes for George. He stood there rocking sideways, back and forth, from foot to foot. He was sweaty and nervous.

Freddie finally looked at George questioningly, then asked, "Wasn't that the day you called and said you weren't feeling well?" he asked George.

George gave a little snicker. Then he slyly said, "Remember, that's the day that Tom wanted different fishing flies. You were there Freddie, at Cabela's"

"Yeah, I was there. Tom was there, but you weren't," Freddie stated. "You called us to say you weren't feeling well. That you would see us Friday if you felt better," Freddie said dryly.

Officer Tuttle and I, in the interim, had walked over to the detective's car. That's when Tuttle said to the detectives, "Just got a cell call from the Naches Ranger Station. They reported on the Thursday afternoon in question at two o'clock, the trailhead security camera showed a man unloading a sleeping bag from the trunk of a car. The car license was clearly seen in the video and when they ran the plates, the car came back registered to a George Ballard."

The officer looked at George and asked, "Aren't you George Ballard?"

George was speechless, looking around like a bear with his foot in a trap. He looked at the officer, then the detectives, and finally asked, "What camera?" He looked around the small parking area, "There's no camera here," he stated with assurance.

"Really?" said Officer Tuttle, then he pointed to the trailhead sign. You could tell the sign was old, but at the very top was a small peephole, it looked newly drilled.

"Sorry, George," the Officer continue, "They installed the camera Wednesday afternoon. Apparently, just in time to watch you doing something suspicious?"

Detective Smith pulled out his cuffs, signaling for George to turn around.

"George Ballard, I'm placing you under arrest on suspicion of murder. Anything you say from here on may be used against you in a court of law. You are entitled to a lawyer. If you can't afford one, one will be provided. Do you understand these rights?"

At that moment, Freddie jumped-in, saying, "George, say yes, and no more. Officers, I'm George's legal representation. You're not to ask him anymore questions. Here is my Bar Association card and number." Freddie pulled a card from his wallet and handed to Detective Smith who read it, wrote the number down, and handed it back to Fred.

As Fred and I watched the detective car pull-out with George fastened in the backseat, handcuffed. Fred said morosely, "Apparently George has the fatal flaw he so gallantly talked of last night."

Me, I was in shock. "Yes, I guess he does," I agreed. "Let's go get our stuff and head home. I don't feel like fishing anymore."

Going Home

The Stetson hat sat atop a small, old suitcase. A kind made of hard cardboard with synthetic leather sewn around the edges and a plastic carrying handle. The hat was a beige hat with an Indian band, dark brown in color, and a turquoise phoenix set in silver at the front. A couple of eagle feathers darted up on one side.

The hat and the case sat there waiting in the hospital hallway, waiting for Jim to go home.

Jim Higgins was in his room also waiting; wondering what was taking her so long. He looked out the window at the hills of Ahtanum Ridge. His love of the land and its people reflected in his clear blue eyes. How long had it been? Eighty years, he thought to himself. No, eighty-two years that he has lived here in the Yakima Valley. He loved this Valley and the only time he left it was to fight in the Pacific. He had returned with a Silver Star; memories, too.

"Can I get you something Mr. Higgins," the nurse asked in her professional but admiring tone. The admiration for Jim Higgins was genuine and full; all the nurses had come to think of Mr. Higgins as their surrogate father. He always had a kind word for everyone and was an easy and cooperative patient. He followed their instruction and his only complaint was the length of his stay. Jim wanted to get back to his ranch. A ranch he had tended his whole life, just as his father before him.

The Higgins Ranch was just outside of Toppenish, about 500 acres on Indian land, which Jim paid for with a small crop share each year. The agent from the Yakama Indian Nation had known the Higgins family most of his life and knew them to be a pioneer ranch family that love the land and respected the local culture. Jim had personally worked with many of the Indian boys to teach them ranch work and had sent a couple to college at his own expense.

Sissy, Jim's daughter, arrived at his room bright and early that morning. Her lithe body showed a little of her 42 years and through good dieting she controlled her weight within ranges that made the family doctor happy. To Jim, his daughter, Sissy, was his whole world. Her smile danced on her lips as her eyes twinkled when she saw him dressed and ready to go. She teased him by saying that the nurse said he had to stay an extra day. He gazed back at her and told her not to tease like that.

About that time a nurse showed-up saying the doctor had written an additional prescription that needed to be picked up down at the pharmacy. "You could do it as you're leaving," she stated.

"Maybe I'll have dad stay here while I go down," Sissy said. "Will that be OK, dad?"

He nodded yes but said to hurry, that he wanted to get back to the ranch before noon.

The Higgins Ranch included a large ranch-styled home, a large red barn, horses, acres, and acres of peach trees. They were some of the best trees in the valley, and, therefore, some of the best in the world.

Jim's family had moved on to this land in 1896 to raise cattle. Switching to peaches was done by Jim's great, great grandfather who like all the Higgins men had that knack to see the future. "Dad, I think James can handle the ranch duties," she said as she left the room.

Jim thought about that a bit. His grandson was very capable, but he always seems to miss some detail or two. He worried about the younger generation and what his grand-children would become. Would they love the ranch and the land as much as he did?

"I hope the pharmacy has the prescription ready," Jim thought and then wondered what it's for?

It started as Jim was waiting by the window thinking about the Indians and their 10,000 years of living off the land. He thought about their annual pow-wows. How the tribes from around Eastern Washington all came together to trade and pow-wow together in Toppenish, a small city in the Yakima Valley. Marriages were also arranged. News was traded as well as horses, baskets and salmon. Even the progress of the white man was noted. 10,000 years, a long time thought Jim.

A slight pain start down Jim's left arm and his upper lip showed a line of sweat just below his well-trimmed mustache, which curled up at each end. Now he could feel a pain deep in his chest and he reached up with his right arm groping for the place. He did not understand what was happening but the Ahtanum Ridge was beginning to turn dark.

* * * * * *

"Code Blue, room 314, Code Blue, Room 314, Code Blue, Room 314," the overhead hospital intercom rang out, crisp and clear.

Sissy was in the pharmacy and didn't quite hear the code call all hospital employees knew was for a patient needing immediate cardiac help. She was just finishing writing the check when the pharmacy girl heard the call for Room 314. "Helen, you need to go to Room 314, code Blue, quickly," she said to a co-worker.

Jim's daughter looked up from writing her check and said, "That's my father's room. "What's the matter," she shouted with urgency. She knew her father was waiting for her upstairs in that very room.

When she got off the elevator, down the hall from her father's room, she saw hospital carts and hospital employees milling around at the door of her father's room, nobody seemed to notice his hat on his suitcase — it too was waiting.

Sissy was about to walk into the room when a nurse grabbed her by the arm and announced herself as the House Supervisor. She guided Sissy down the hall to a waiting area. "Does your dad have a non-recessitate order on file," she asked Sissy? Sissy had started to cry but now she stopped and thought for a moment. She remembered that dad had always said that when the time came for his trail to end that he didn't want a lot of heroics. "Did he," the Supervisor kept asking?

Collecting her thoughts for a moment, Sissy suddenly felt alone, yet, she needed to make a clear decision about what her father wanted. She wished her brother were here instead of off fishing somewhere. Maybe she could reach her son who had been busy at the ranch when she left.

"I know he didn't want heroics at the end," she replied to the nurse through tears. She could hardly speak and felt woozy and numb. A nurse handed her some Kleenex and gave Sissy a small paper cup of water.

Meanwhile, hospital people were going in and out of her father's room quickly; a doctor shouted for blood pressure readings, gave a quick order for the paddles and then someone shouted, "CLEAR!"

The House Supervisor told Sissy that she might want to call the family.

"But, I'm here to take him home," replied Sissy, helplessly.

"I know, but things happen," the nurse replied gently. The nurse was gentle but firm in telling Sissy again to call family. She was saying at his age one could never be sure what would happen. Then she hastily ran down the hall and into Sissy's father's room.

At the same time, another nurse took her place beside Sissy and gently held Sissy's arm. She was quietly telling her that Jim was having difficulty but that they may be able to keep him going until family arrived.

It was then that the Higgins strength kicked in and Sissy realized that she had to think about her father in realist terms. She thought about his suffering until family arrived, if they could even get to the hospital in time, and what purpose would that serve. "No," she said softly. "No, don't let him suffer. Make him comfortable and let God take His course. That is what Dad would want; it would make sense to him."

The nurse nodded and rushed off only to be replaced by another nurse who bent down to tell her the team was doing everything it was trained to do.

The nurse supervisor returned and asked Sissy what religion she preferred, if any. Sissy looked up from her Kleenex and said that daddy was Catholic and would like Absolution if possible.

A call immediately went to the hospital clergyman that a priest needed to be sent to Room 314 stat.

In the room, the team was performing with a cold precision; nurses and doctors calling out instructions and status to each other in a meticulous well-rehearsed routine of a Code Blue. The pupils are dilated and set, someone called out. Time is eleven forty-three.

Sissy sat with tears in her eyes and the box of Kleenex on her lap, thinking of the times Dad had come through the front door of their ranch house, swooped her into his strong arms, giving her a big wet kiss on the cheek. She remembers his trembling when mom had died. How he had wept openly and said how much his wife of 52 years had meant to him. She thought about her son's birth and remembered dad's thrill when she announced he had a grandson. She remembered last Christmas, the first without their mother.

"I'm so sorry," a nurse said quietly. "We did all we could." Sissy just nodded and thanked her quietly. The Nurse Supervisor told Sissy that the staff was preparing him if she waited a few moments to visit it would be helpful. "OK," Sissy said weakly, her red eyes clouded with tears, the Kleenex at her nose.

As she sat there, she looked down the hospital hallway to Room 314. Right outside the door in the hallway was Jim Higgins' Stetson hat still sitting atop his small, battered suitcase. Sissy noted the hat showed signs of wear and some sweat stains just above the band. The little suitcase was scratched and damaged in several places. Sissy had always planned to replace it.

Now, both just sat there, waiting.

Fletches Time

This morning, Brad sits, waiting. His rugged good looks give not a hint of his inner turmoil. He sits erect, his full head of hair is dark with slight graying at the temples, a mustache that matches the darkness of his hair is combed downward in a broom fashion, and each bristle is perfectly in place.

He reaches for his coffee and says aloud, "This is for shit." He brings the mug to his lips and sips the coffee, not allowing it to touch his mustache. He wishes the coffee were hotter and stronger.

Brad is wiry and quick of movement. When at work, he makes quick decision and moves fast because of both his experience and training. Once he makes a decision, he rarely changes it. Stubborn, would come to mind.

"Hate this, shit," he murmurs, again, over his coffee mug. "Hate this." His eyes narrow and are more like slits which miss little and when you talk with him, it is then his eyes open up enough for you to see they are green.

He sits his mug down on the end table, then slides back on to the couch, and folds his strong arms. He has a defiant air. He has something that he needs to do, but really does not want to do it.

The front door bell rings and Brad is quick to jump up and answer the ring by opening door.

There, standing at the door, is Dave, Brad's fishing buddy. In fact, they have been friends for over thirty years. Each had been in the war and after they got out, they met when both went to work at the same body shop. Fifteen years ago, Brad left the body shop for a management position with a trucking firm. Dave and Brad remain strong friends; going fishing every chance Brad can sneak away.

"He's doing better," Brad states before Dave can enter. "He's do'in much better," Brad accents "much" and then adds quickly, "I think we should wait."

Dave knows his friend. He doesn't answer quickly. He waits a moment or two, then asks, "Brad, what about tonight?" He waits, again, before adding, "It going to be cold, again, tonight."

Brad grabs his mug and goes to sit down then decides to stand. "Get yourself some coffee." He doesn't want to answer the question. He moves about like an animal trapped in a cage. He's like cat pacing back and forth.

"I hate this, Dave," Brad says, looking for a way to stop it. "I think we should wait," then pauses, then, adds, "Ah, shit! You're right, the nights are the worst. Shit, this is just shit." Dave sees that Brad is struggling with himself.

"Settle down, Brad," Dave encourages his friend. "You're doing the right thing." Dave watches as Brad paces, stops, and then goes into the kitchen. He hears the coffee mug hit the counter and then fall into the sink.

Man this guy is over the edge, he thinks to himself. Then out-loud Dave says, "Let's rock and roll, Big Guy. We need to move out."

Brad pauses, then, goes to the garage door saying, "Yeah, let's go." He opens the door and looks out. "Fletch, where are you ol' boy?"

The cold wind snaps through the open door as Brad steps into the garage. Dave follows quickly, each looking for Fletch. There, standing uncertain in the front part of the garage, by the metal door, is Fletch. He shakes and tries to look better than his deteriorated condition. His hips are stiff and his hind legs hardly move. When they do move, one can see the pain that radiates through his body. His head hangs as his big brown eyes question what is wrong. Looking at Brad,

Fletch gives just the end of his thin tail a shake to show he is happy to see his master.

Two years ago, Fletch would have been up and at the kitchen door in an instant, tail wagging mightily, a haughty little bark of excitement, nose up, eyes bright, looking forward to the love pat and a wonderful first meal of the day.

Brad would have poured out the food and refreshed his water. And, then as Fletch ate, Brad would have given him a stroke of his hand down his back and said have a good day, ol' boy.

Not today. Those happy days of meeting each morning are over. Replaced by time's ever-marching pace in which only one reality exists: change.

Change is the only certainty in life. Of which, death and decay is the ultimate consequence. Change has caught up with Fletch, and with Brad. Brad hates it; Fletch doesn't understand it, each struggle with the situation.

Brad brightens, saying, "Jesus, Dave he looks much better today!"

Pretending not to hear, Dave asks, "Where's his leash?"

"Don't have one. Maybe, we should go get one," Brad answers, hoping Dave will see wisdom in doing this.

Dave looks around the garage. He notices a laundry type rope piled on Brad's workbench. "What's wrong with using that piece of rope right there?" he asks, pointing at the rope. "It will tie to his collar." Dave hardly noticed the dark cloud pass over Brad's face.

Brad moved quickly over to the rope, cutting off Dave before he could reach it. "I'll do it," he said with resignation. "I'll do it."

He picked up the white rope and walked over to Fletch. As Fletch sat on the cold concrete, he looked up at his master with big, questioning eyes. A shot of pain shook his body and he bowed his head slightly.

Brad inserted the rope under the collar and then tied a knot. Checking the knot, he said, "OK, ol' boy, let's go" as he gently urged Fletch up.

One could see the effort, one could sense the determination, and one could feel Fletches need to obey his master's request. With a mighty heave and a deep, painful breath, he began the effort to raise his hips from the concrete.

His legs shook and wavered, he struggle to control them, to bring them into compliance. He sucked in another breath as the pain tore throw him. He bent his front legs a bit, took a deep breath, and pushed his entire body up and with effort came the hips. For a second, his triumph was complete. His eyes, for a split second, brightened, his master's wish was fulfilled.

From the terrible reality appeared the truth, and, yes, the inevitable. It started at his back paws, sliced up his legs and exploded in his hips. The discharge flashed up his backbone and then detonated down his front legs.

His eyes closed and one could hear his breath escape in a hiss. The body shook a second, then, began to crumble back to the concrete. There he lay dazed, stunned, and unable to comprehend what had just taken place in his body, a body that had served him well for so long. He looked to his master for an answer.

Seeing his pain, Brad reached down to try to help his long-time companion but to no avail. Fletch hit the garage floor hard and whimpered his pain. Brad said aloud, really to no one, "Shit, poor guy can't even stand."

"Brad, you better carry him," Dave stated almost as a command. Dave's eyes were watery and his sadness inside welled-up. End of life is never pretty for those left behind.

Perhaps, when we see our future, it hurts. He could see a tear in Brad's eye as Brad knelt down to pick up Fletch.

With desolation, Dave reached for Fletches pillow. "I got his pillow," Dave said quietly. "We can put him in the back of truck."

It was a cold day. Dave put the pillow in the bed of the truck, making sure it was centered towards the front under the rear window of the truck. He wanted to reduce any wind that might cause Fletch problems.

"Don't worry about the wind," Brad said, noting what Dave was trying to do. He appreciated the concern his best friend showed and was grateful he was here.

"Maybe I should just hold him on my lap?" Braid said.

"No," Dave replied. "He might have an accident and I don't want it where I can't wash it out. He'll be OK in the back."

"Yeah, he loves to smell the wind," Brad said, recalling how Fletch would stick his head out the car window to take in the wind.

"I got the biggest kick how he would sniff the wind," remembering a time or two when Fletch would lift his nose in the wind and take in deep breaths. He remembered how Fletch would smell something important and duck back into the vehicle and bark and whimper like Brad should immediately stop the car and let him out to investigate. When Brad would tell him to settle down, Fletch would jump back to the armrest with his front paws and stick his head back out the window, smelling for the next interesting scent.

Brad was sitting in the cab of the truck as they drove to the vets, telling Dave how much he was going to miss his best friend. He kept looking out the back window to make sure that Fletch was safe and to watch him as he struggled to lift his nose to the wind.

"God, Dave, he is a great dog," Brad stated with emotion. "I'll miss the hell out of him."

Dave, watching the road, glanced quickly at his friend and then back to the road. "Remember the time he smelled that skunk out in your back yard. What a damn mess. He chased that poor bastard in behind the shed, didn't he?"

"Hell, yes," Brad brightened. He thought a moment, and then smiled, "Got his ass sprayed, too. Didn't stop him, though. Went right in and killed that varmint, he remembered. "Took me a week to get rid of the smell and hundreds dollar worth of vet bills to patch his ass up," Brad laughed at the thought of it. A few minutes passed before Brad asked, "Remember the time I had that burglar in my back yard. It was about three in the morning when he came over the fence. Fletch heard him and was on him like stink on shit. Guy never had a firkin chance.

Brad went on for about ten minutes with how Fletch and the burglar faced off with each other. Brad saw the guy from the bedroom window take a couple of swings with some kind of wench before Fletch caught him in the lower calve of his leg. Brad had turned away from the window to call the police and when they got there, they found a trail of blood leading from the middle of the yard back to the fence where the person must have jumped back over.

"Police said Fletch must of bit a hole clean through the asshole's leg," Brad said with pride. "Never caught the sum'bitch though. Ole' Fletch, hell of a dog."

Brad had retreated back into his memories when Dave intruded by saying, "Well, we're here."

Brad looked up to see the vet's office and a welcoming sign that cautioned all pets must be on a leash. "Shit, we've only got a rope," Brad said loudly, almost happy they didn't have a leash.

Looking at his friend's hopefulness, he answered, "They'll be just fine with the rope. Want me to go in and make the arrangements?"

Brad gave a nod, and then stepped out of the cab and turned to Fletch as Dave went into the Vet's office. He stoked Fletches back as his failing canine friend lay in the bed of the truck. "You were a great dog," he said, then added, "I'll miss you, Fletch." Tears filled his eyes as his strong arms and hands continued to stroke his canine pal.

Dave came back out and announced all was ready. "I explained the situation, Brad," he said. "They said you've made a good decision, that it's best for Fletch." He paused to wait for an acknowledgement, but none came. Brad continued to stroke Fletches back for a few moments. Dave noted Brad's shoulder shake a bit, then tremble. He put his hand on Brad's shoulder and gave a squeeze to let his friend know he was there for him. Moments passed.

Suddenly, Brad took a deep breath and said to Dave, "Carry him in, I can't do it."

Dave squeezed his friend's shoulder once more, looked at Fletch lying on the pillow. Fletch was quiet now, almost as if he knew his fate and had resigned himself to it. Dave reached into the bed of the truck and carefully picked up Fletch and drew him into his arms. As he held him to his chest, Brad removed the rope from his collar and threw it into the truck bed. Then he grabbed the side of the truck bed for support and look out into the distance. This was Dave's cue and he wasted no time turning and heading into the vet's office.

As he went through the front door, the older lady behind the check-in counter stood up. She took one quick look at Fletch, pointed down the hallway and commanded, "Down the hall, first door on the right. Pick any cage and put him in. Lock the cage after you have him in."

Dave didn't hesitate. Down the hall he went, Fletch in arms. He was surprised how heavy Fletch had become and was wasting no time in this grim task. Once in the holding room, he looked for a cage. Finding one on the bottom row, he quickly knelt and carefully laid Fletch in it. Locking the cage door, Dave avoided looking at Fletch and thought to himself that he wanted to remember him as he was before this terrible time.

Once the cage locked, he turned and went to leave. But he did look back at Fletch, and with tears in his eyes, said under his breath with remorse, "Damn it!" He walked out into the hall, stonily looking ahead, back to the front waiting area.

At the counter, Brad was preparing to write-out a check while he was telling Fletch stories. He was telling the two ladies behind the counter how Fletch had one time tried to jump a six foot cyclone fence and had come up short. "God, he had a butt full of wire stuck in his chest," he nervously laughed. "I think it cost me about two hundred bucks to get him sown up." He thought a moment, and then added, "He was right out there the next week jumping that same fence. Made it over every time, I had to add two more feet to stop him. Great dog! Great dog!"

The two women agreed with him, then looked at each other knowingly. The older woman asked if Fletch had sired any pups.

"Don't know, for sure," Brad answered with some thought. "Ya' know he mostly jumped that fence in the springtime. Maybe he was the stud of the neighborhood," he said with a show of male pride. "There were a couple of younger dogs that certainly looked like him. Who's to say?" Then he asked quickly, "What do I owe you?"

* * * * *

In the truck, on their way back to Brad's house neither man spoke for a long time. Each seemed to be content with the hum of the engine and being lost in their thoughts.

Dave thought about his friend and the turmoil he would go through until he adjusted to life without Fletch.

Brad was thinking he didn't want to forget Fletches pillow in the back of the truck.

Finally, Brad said aloud, "They asked me if I wanted a paw print." The statement hung there for a moment as Dave digested the comment and Brad waited for a reaction.

"Uh, great idea, Brad," Dave finally coughed out. "Yeah, good," he added, wanting to sound supportive. Paw print, he contemplated. "Good God. What will you do with that Brad," he thought? "So, when will it be ready?" he asked Brad.

"Hmm, about two weeks they said. Picking up his ashes, too." Then he added, "Bought an urn, also.

"You bought an urn?" Dave questioned. He thought this is a side of Brad I've never seen. "Wow," He exclaimed.

"Yep, probably bury it in the back yard somewhere," Brad said with pomp. "Fletch deserves that much for being the great dog he was."

* * * * *

Back in his house, Brad decides he needs another cup of hot coffee. In the kitchen, he realizes he has left the Mr. Coffee pot on and that the coffee is still hot. "Guess it doesn't take that long to put an old-friend down," he thinks. Now he finds his cup in the sink, rinses it out, and refills it. Looking out into the backyard, somehow it's different. Empty, it feels empty now that Fletch is gone.

This morning is almost over as Brad sits thinking of his canine friend. His rugged good looks give not a hint of his inner turmoil. He sits erect, his full head of hair is still dark with slight graying at the temples, a mustache that matches the darkness of his hair is still combed downward in a broom fashion, and each bristle is still perfectly in place.

He reaches for his coffee and says aloud, "This morning is for shit." He brings the mug to his lips and sips the coffee, not allowing it to touch his mustache. He wishes the coffee were fresher and hotter, and stronger.

And, as Brad sips his coffee, Fletches eyes grow heavy, his body relaxes, and his soul gracefully achieves the impartation to eternity.

The Mystery of Curly Simmons

I don't really remember the first time I saw Curly. He has just been a part of my memory for my entire life, not an important part, but a part that reminds you of what you don't want to become. Curly was one of those people you never really knew much about, but it seemed you've known him forever. He was always there, waiting, and talking, and watching. He was soft-spoken, always polite and quick to say something nice even if you didn't always understand him. Dad would always say what a shame Curly's a drunk.

Curly's eyes were the one feature I remember as being his most outstanding physical quality. His eyes were clear blue, not a deep blue, but, rather, a pale, soft blue, clear like the sky, with a black dot dead center. They were sad eyes, ones that had experienced deep-sorrow, ones which saw humanity at its worst and ones that had seen the best life had to offer. Intelligence also showed in his eyes. Those intelligent eyes could look directly into your soul and knew if you had something happening in your life, be it happy or sad. His eyes contrasted against his tan, ruddy face and he combed his hair straight back. In his later years a bald spot would develop, but he was determined to comb his thinning hair straight back.

My father was a merchant, a member of the merchant class in the middle of the recovery after World War II. His retail outlet was a liquor store in South Central Los Angeles and Curly Simmons was one of his most consistent customers if not a big spender. Cheap Santa Fe White Port was his choice of drink. He drank it incessantly from morning to night, trying to erase from his memory some dreadful event, or, perhaps, he was trying to escape the pain of a life's shattering loss.

Dad told me how Curly would be waiting at the front door of the store every morning at seven-thirty to purchase his first "pony" of White Port. He'd paid Dad with loose change that he had either found or begged from people. He was good at panhandling.

His filthy hands would shake as he laid out his change on the counter. When he pushed the money across the counter, you would have to turn your head away to avoid his early morning breath. And, he'd always come up a penny or two short.

As a kid, I remember Dad saying, "Curly, you're short three cents." Dad would pause and wait while Curly searched through his pockets for some additional change. Dad knew Curly would have nothing to add. After what to Curly must have seemed eons, Dad would say firmly, "Bring it back later."

Curly would begin thanking Dad so profusely, he would begin to spit, his lips would pucker and his eyes watered—it was as if this was the greatest kindness that ever had happened to him. Then Dad would place the pony of wine in a narrow sack specifically designed for wine bottles while reminding Curly to be careful.

On Monday nights my mother, my sister and I would bring Dad his dinner sometime between five and six. While Dad ate in the tiny office, which also doubled kitchen, mom would wait the counter. I would be assigned to sweep the parking lot while my sister helped our mother.

One Monday night I was out sweeping the lot when Curly came around the corner from the alley side of the lot. He was dressed in his usual tan khaki pants and a summer short-sleeved shirt. His black shoes were tattered and scuffed beyond belief. One was missing a heel. Curley was staggering a bit. He was drunk but could walk with effort. When he saw me, he hesitated for moment, then, waved for me to come over.

"Can you help?" he said, pausing for a moment to sort out his thoughts. Then he continued, "I need three more cents to get somethun' to drin...uh somethun' to eat."

I told him I didn't have any money. He said he understood and began looking around the parking lot for someone else to help him. He spotted a battered truck that had just pulled up. The driver was a redneck (you know the type, close-cut hair, big, muscular arms, tattoos, dirty and loud) with his girl-friend seated thigh to thigh with him.

Curly staggered over to them, politely excused himself, and then tried to explain his needing a few more cents for a sandwich.

"A sandwich, huh?" the redneck replied. Then he turned to his girlfriend and said, "Watch this!"

He searched his pockets and brought out some change, which he threw at Curly. The coins hit Curly in the face.

This made Curly jump back as the change scattered all over the ground. He stood there in a stupor for a moment, before he realized the redneck had given him money. Stooping over, he to started picking up the scattered coins, thanking the redneck all the while.

The redneck watched Curly lower himself to the ground. Then he opened his truck door fast and hard, which hit Curly with a callous thud, knocking him to the pavement. The redneck jumped out of the truck and pushed Curly just as Curly was trying to get up.

"Get the fuck out of my way you fucking wino!" he yelled at Curly, all the while looking back at his girlfriend. Then he hit Curly in the face with his big, meaty fist.

Curly went down on his back and I could see blood coming from his nose. The redneck driver went into the store like nothing happened.

Curly lay still for a moment with blood gushing from his nose. I could see his left eye had received part of the blow. I was frozen in place, not believing what I had just witnessed.

Then Curly rolled over on to his hands and knees and began again to look for the change, crawling around the parking lot with blood still dripping from his face. Occasionally he whimpered. I stood there not accepting the truth, that the money could be that important.

When the redneck came back out of the store with two six-packs of Coors, he saw Curley crawling on hands and knees searching for money.

"Still needing money, asshole?" he yelled down at Curly. "Here, take this." And he held out a dollar bill.

When Curly shakily reached up for it, the redneck kicked him in the stomach, sending poor Curly to the pavement once again, this time withering in pain. He looked at Curly, then, at his girlfriend who was laughing.

The redneck dangled the dollar bill in a questioning manner.

The girlfriend yelled, "Goddamn it Artie, give it to him!" Artie dropped the dollar bill on the ground next to Curly. Then he hopped into his truck. His girlfriend laughed and stroked her beau's arm and kissed him. "Come on, Big Boy, let's go have some fun," she said in a tantalizing playful manner, as she reached into his lap.

As the truck rolled out of the lot, it almost ran over Curly who had grabbed the dollar bill with his dirty hand and was trying courageously to get up.

He jumped out of harm's way just in time, but then fell again. I ran over to help him up but he said, "You'd better go inside." Curly just laid there.

"Go on, now," He said nobly, a dirty hand clutching the precious dollar. "Get inside."

At the store's door, I looked back and there Curly was trying to pick up a penny he had missed earlier. I guess every cent counts no matter what level of society you're at. I took one final glance back. He waved me inside and I went to put the broom away.

When I returned to the front counter there was Curly, black-eyed with caked-on blood. He was paying for a fifth of Santa Fe. It was a big score, and he was going to celebrate his victory.

* * * * *

The years rolled by and I graduated from high school and attended a year of college before entering the Air Force.

In the early sixties, the Vietnam War was just beginning to heat-up and I expected to go there. However, Fate stepped in and I was assigned to a base in Japan, where I spent three years learning about the Japanese, and enjoyed touring the country on my off-duty time.

After my first year in the Far East, I returned home for a thirty-day leave. I was visiting the employees at my Dad's store when Curly came through the front door. He was walking straight and had cleaned up. He stopped at the counter, stood there for a moment looking at me, trying to focus and also find the right words to welcome me home.

"You're home," he finally said. He weaved a bit and took a drag on his Camel.

His fingers were burnt and yellow from smoking every last cigarette down to the last quarter inch. "I am glad," he added as he pinched the butt between his fingers.

I noted his watery blue eyes and the redness of his lids. I was aware of the yellowish hue to his skin and in the whites of his eyes; both indicators of liver failure. I worried for him.

"Yep, I'm home, Curly," I responded. "How are ya doing?"

He looked at me for a moment standing there in my air force uniform, then said, "I was in the war, too."

"Really," I said; then teasingly, "Was that World War One?" He looked at me blankly, not quite knowing how to respond, saying finally and simply, "Omaha Beach."

It was as though he wanted me to know, yet, was trying to forget all at the same time. The sadness that came over him, I'll never forget.

The beaten down man withdrew into himself for a long moment and then blurted out, "Really glad you're OK."

"Me, too, Curly, me too," I said to him softly, wishing I hadn't teased.

He reached a trembling hand inside his old blue sweater which was buttoned-up to his chest over his checkered shirt, out came his Camels.

He even motioned towards me to ask if I wanted one, a supreme jester coming from Curly because he had probably panhandled for a couple hours to get the change to buy that pack of smokes.

When I shook my head no, he turned and went to the wine shelves, picked up a pony of his White Port and returned to the counter.

As he was reaching into his tan khaki pants pockets for some change, I pulled a bag from under the counter to wrap the bottle and told him this one's on me.

He stood there for a wobbly moment, clutching the wrapped bottle in his stained hands searching for the right words.

"Th..th..thanks," he stuttered. As he left the store, he called back quietly, "You be careful over there."

That was the last I would see of Curly until I returned home for my final time. I got home two years later and Curly was in a wheelchair.

* * * * *

When I completed my military service, I returned home with the intention of completing my college education. I enrolled in a junior college and later transferred to a university.

My field of interest was international studies; I wanted to become a CIA spook. As fate would have it though, I switched to accounting and business, in which I excelled.

It was early in my junior college days when dad shared with me some things Curly had told him.

Dad told me that Curly no longer drank, that he was dry, and had kicked the booze.

Why?

Because he'd slipped off the curb of a street in a drunken stupor and had broken his back. Curly was now a paraplegic and couldn't use his legs.

He told Dad that the paramedics were making bets that he wouldn't last the week out. It scared Curly. He got help from Social Security and the Daughters of Charity Mission. He hadn't taken a sip of wine since the mishap.

"Gosh, Dad, sounds like Curly really opened up to you?" I asked.

"Yes, he did," Dad replied and then said, "He told me about a woman, too. Apparently, she died a couple years after he returned from overseas, from France. A car accident, I think. Curly wasn't really clear about that."

"Curly has never been clear," I quipped.

"Son, don't judge a man until you have walked some in his shoes," My dad said. Dad always found the good in a person, even Curly.

My life suddenly changed one Friday afternoon when mom called to say dad had suffered a heart attack. He was in the community hospital, and it was serious.

I called into my part-time accounting job and told them I wouldn't be in. It turned out I never returned to the job, or school, because dad passed away that evening and my life changed forever.

Dad and I had a few moments together before his final attack. We exchanged small talk, both of us not believing he wouldn't recover. As it turned out, it was a day I never really recovered from. I just adjusted to the change. Some people never adjust; like Curly they just go hide.

* * * * *

Not long after Dad's funeral, I was clerking the store when a customer named Carl came in, drunk, and began to babble about what a great person my dad was.

"Your dad was a peach of a guy," Carl slurred.

I replied, "Yes, I think so, too."

About that time, Curly come wheeling-in in his chair with a Camel hanging out his mouth. I hadn't seen much of Curly since my homecoming and I was impressed how great he looked compared with the old Curly.

"Curly," I waved. "Lookin' good, my man!"

Curly looked back at me and gave a quick wave when he noticed Carl standing at the counter.

I thought I detected a groan as he wheeled down an aisle to get some soda pop. Carl looked at Curley with contempt and leaned over the counter and said, "Why didn't God take that piece of shit instead of your old man?"

I saw Curly's neck stiffen a bit, but he said nothing and continued to the cooler. Carl just looked at me waiting for a reply.

Not really wanting to validate his comment, I replied, "That's not a nice thing to say, Carl."

"Sure it is," Carl loudly said back to me as he leaned over the counter. "Curly is worthless, a life wasted. Your old man helped everybody. What kind of God takes a decent man like him and keeps people like dipshit Curly alive?"

I had bent over to get a pack of matches. When I straightened up, there was Curly, in his wheelchair, behind the inebriated Carl, who was busy making an ass of his self.

I gave Carl his book of matches and thanked him for shopping with us, and "to have a pleasant night." As he left, he turned to Curly, talking from the corner of his mouth, said, "Why couldn't it have been you, you prick?" He walked out of the store without turning back. Curly just sat there.

We must have sat there for a moment or two, and then I said, "Curly, God has a plan for all of us. Some people don't understand that."

"I know," he said quietly, "Your dad was a decent man."

He paid for his soda pop and a pack of Camels. I watched him wheel his chair out the door, knowing it took great effort, but amazed he was one of few who got off booze and was able to stay off it.

Over the next years, I saw Curly regularly. He never drank. He never confided in me anything else about himself. And, he always wore his tattered blue sweater and always smoked his Camels.

* * * * *

Several years after dad died, when I was in my early thirties, I sold the business and moved my family to a small, provincial town.

Curly was at the store on my last day--in his wheelchair--smoking his Camels to their last quarter inch-- as I helped the new owners to acclimate to the business.

Curley told me he was sad about the change but wished me well. Within minutes he was out in the parking lot—panhandling; only this time he really was going to buy food. I guess old habits are hard to change.

A year or two after we sold the business I heard from a former customer that Curly had passed away. He was found in his tattered, old blue sweater, lying next to a Stradivarius violin and an old Kodak picture of a beautiful woman who had signed it, "To My main squeeze, whom I love with all my heart-forever." The black and white picture was dated 1949. With it was a Purple Heart and Bronze Star with two clusters.

Also in the violin case was a music score from the New York Philharmonic Orchestra dated 1947, autographed by the great Leonard Bernstein. This man, Curly Simmons, whose smoke stained fingers and filthy fingernails, had once used those same fingers to create the beauty of Chopin, Beethoven, Mozart and Brahms on his classic violin.

Thus, was the mystery of Curly Simmons, a tragic figure; who had musical talent; who had loved; who had turned to alcohol for what; comfort, escape, or something unfathomable from the war?

Mozart once said, "Most men go their grave with most of their music in them." To this day, I wonder just how much music Curly took with him.

Corner Warriors

On any given morning, on any given day, and on any given corner you may see one of them; solitary, downtrodden, seemingly beaten by the world. They stand there, almost perfectly still, looking down at the sidewalk. Others rock gently from foot to foot; they too look down at the sidewalk. It's as if they've all been coached by the same mentor.

Under their scruffy chins, they hold a sign pleading for a donation using a varying of catchphrases: "Please Help"; "DOWN on my luck"; "homeless"; "$1 will help"; "anything helps"; "N E E D help"; "my wife had a better lawyer". All end with "God Bless". Rather, most all ends with god bless, except for the one with the lousy lawyer — his ended with "Lucky Me".

Some mendicants are young, but most are older, fifty and beyond. Some are clean-shaven, but most have long gray beards. Some have shaved heads, but most have long straggly graying locks that hang onto their shoulders. All are in tattered, dirty clothes.

In winter they wear frayed coats, fingerless gloves, and moth-eaten, scruffy knitted caps some old ladies weaved, then, donated to the local mission.

All are disheveled masses of humanity living at the very edge of society. All, except for the one with the lousy lawyer, although he's about to be evicted from his motel apartment unless he can come up with rent money.

All are standing a street corner just hoping a rare driver heralds a willingness to hand over some loose change. Or, if the driver's benevolent side so cajoles them, maybe they'll free-up a dollar, or a Lincoln, or maybe, with real luck, a Hamilton; although "anything will help."

It's at the corner of First Street and Nob Hill Boulevard you will find the celebrated chieftain of the Corner Warriors, Chief Kamiakin.

The man standing the corner isn't of Indian ancestry. He doesn't even resemble an Indian but the local population, nevertheless, has come to call him that. Even the local Yakama Indians call him Chief Kamiakin because of his persistent nature and staunchness like their actual legendary chief.

The real Chief Kamiakin is considered the last true hero of the Yakama Indian Nation. The current chief has trained most all the present day panhandlers.

Today's Chief Kamiakin works his corner like dedicated men work their jobs, with devotion and perseverance. He's been panhandling on the same corner for so many years he has become a fixture in the city of Yakima. Citizens on their way to work, who miss seeing him because he's on a break, or at lunch, have been known to actually check their calendars to make sure they haven't overlooked a holiday.

In the warmer months, April through October, the Chief takes his stand very early in the morning, no later than seven. Usually a few minutes before seven each working day, he comes from behind the dumpster situated at the back of the city's first McDonald's, arranges his backpack, then faces the traffic going west to work. Once there, he places his sign under his chin, and gives a hesitant little smile, and patiently waits his first benefactor.

Long before panhandling became a way of life for many street people, Chief Kamiakin was the sole person with his sign out, working the corners of his choosing. He had his choice of corners throughout the small city. Some say he tried out other busy corners, but found he had his best luck at First and Nob Hill. The city's traffic count showed that particular corner had the highest traffic counts in the city.

The Chief knew exactly what he was staking out without ever reading the official traffic counts.

The Chief was a real pro. He always held his sign in place for the exact length of a red signal—never more, never less. His timing was impeccable.

Without looking, he would bring his handmade sign down, turn his back on the moving traffic and retrace his steps to his backpack for a drink out of his water bottle.

Just before more traffic was stopped by the next red light, Kamiakin had put his bottle away, positioned his backpack, and resumed his position, facing the traffic, which was rolling to a stop.

With his sign in its proper position, he would face the new set of drivers and give them a brief, timorous grin, sometimes even tossing in a weak wave.

Occasionally, to break the monotony of standing in one place, he would slowly shuffle up the sidewalk, infrequently glancing up from the sidewalk but never really focusing on any one car.

When Chief shuffled even with your car, he might give you a transitory glance, then, immediately his eyes dropped back to the sidewalk. Don't ask me how, but he instinctively detected when a driver was about to offer a donation. While working this coy gamesmanship, he was sensitive to a driver's body language and was quick to receive the contribution, then, mumble something that amount to a strained thank-you.

People who tried to engage him in conversation were disappointed. Once, a minister invited him to his church services on Sunday. Chief gave his little smile, nodded, grabbed the bequest from the preacher's hand, and coldly return to the sidewalk.

He even knew just how long a green light would last and at what precise time he needed to turn back to the corner for the next red light. Just before the current red light would turn green, he would stop his slow progression; pull down his sign and start a jaunty walk back to the corner, arriving there just in time for the next red signal.

If he was fortunate enough to have a donor, somehow he would collect his prize and still be able to return safely to the corner for the next round.

And, so Chief made his way through life panhandling, working his corner diligently; never wavering in his commitment. People respect commitment.

During the warm months of the year, he was at his corner every work day.

And in winter, if the day was forecast to be mild, he would appear. He worked his day the same every day: start at seven, morning break at ten, and lunch from noon to two.

Chief had figured out over the years that people didn't like to take time to donate during lunch, and he also realized many people started heading home around two in the afternoon.

But as the years passed, and Chief Kamiakin worked his magic, the world changed.

The Yakima city council built a new jail to house prisoners sent over from Seattle, plus the economy turned negative. More and more hard-working people were thrown out of work. Many started losing their homes, while corporate America was making record profits.

The trickle of money to the lower-income folks shrank mightily. Prisoners released from that new county jail weren't given enough money or required to return to Seattle. Many, in fact most, were not employable material. Soon many of them were indigent and homeless, adding to the depressed economy of Yakima.

But none of this affected the Chief. He worked his corner, positioning his sign just so under his chin, shuffling up the street a bit, giving a fleeting smile and tenuous wave. He collected his donations (which were becoming scarcer), mumbled his thanks, but always he took his breaks.

Then, on one blustery morning break it happened.

It was the Chief's habit to take his early break at ten every morning. He reasoned workers at that time of the morning would take their breaks, but few would drive anywhere. They would stay at their work sites and drink coffee, have a donut, or enjoy some food brought from home. Therefore, he reasoned, this was the time for him to go the McDonald's and get a small coffee of his own.

After purchasing it, he would return to his place behind the restaurant's dumpster and relax with his back against the container to have a smoke and drink his coffee.

On this fateful day, Chief returned with his coffee. As he rounded the corner of the dumpster to assume his regular place, he unexpectedly encountered a person already seated with his back against the dumpster, smoking and drinking his own coffee.

Chief Kamiakin stopped, held his coffee for a long moment—he didn't quite know what to do.

As he hesitated, the stranger turned and looked up at him. He gave a smile, a sheepish smile, one that said, "Here I am, hope it's alright?"

"What?" Chief finally and nervously blurted out.

The stranger jumped up quickly and stuck a hand out to the Chief. "Howdy," he said loudly.

Chief Kamiakin recoiled in fear, taking a step back and turning away. His eyes followed the stranger's hand, never for one second taking them off the extended limb. Maybe he thought the stranger was grabbing for his coffee.

Whatever it was, whatever he thought, the chief was not comfortable. His action made this apparent to the stranger.

The stranger lowered his hand slowly as Chief continued to watch the hand as it moved away.

Taking a step backwards himself, the foreigner said, "Hey, I don't mean you any harm." He paused a moment before adding, "I was hoping you could help me?"

"Help you?" Chief repeated, standing back from the strange man, eyes still glued to the man's hand. He took a quick glance at the man's heavy beard, his long dark hair that dangled to the man's shoulder, and his clothes.

Then his eyes returned back to the stranger's hand.

Chief note the stranger's clothes were high quality, but dirty and rumpled. The stranger's smile was large and imposing, making Chief more uncomfortable and suspicious.

Chief stood there, coffee in hand, a blank look which conveyed no understanding of what was happening. The gregarious stranger remained standing, not sure what to say or do next. Chief continued to look at the hand that had been extended in friendship.

Unspoken but understood, the stranger then made a special effort to hold his coffee cup with both hands not to further alarm Chief.

Quietly, he said, "My name is Bill." Bill waited a moment, then, slowly held out his hand again.

Chief Kamiakin looked at the man's outstretched hand, apprehension flowed through his body, his eyes remained fixed on Bill's hand in fear. His eyes followed it again as the stranger lowered it once again.

"What's with you, Chief?" Bill grunted, perplexed.

When Bill used Chief's name, Chief had looked up from Bill's hand and stared into Bill's deep-set eyes. Surprise set-in, replacing fear. The stranger knew his name. And, once again, the stranger was sitting down, resting his back against Chief Kamiakin's dumpster. "Is he staying?" Chief asked himself?

"This is my place," Chief Kamiakin stated resolutely. Uncomfortable, Chief fidgets, then, he repeats, "This is my place."

Chief hovered there, half expecting the man to leave. He stared down at the man as Bill adjusted himself against the trash receptacle. He was telling Kamiakin to join him if he wanted. The chief began to rock from foot to foot, still not comprehending what the stranger was up to.

Finally, he announced once again, "This is my place." Kamiakin waited for the stranger to answer, and when he didn't, Chief repeated himself, only a little louder, "This is my spot!" He stepped forward menacingly, towards the stranger. The disheveled stranger didn't seem to notice, or care.

Finally, Bill looked up at Chief, patted the ground next to him, and ordered Chief to sit down. "Sit down, right here, right now," Bill commanded him.

Chief stared at the hand as it patted the ground next to the stranger. He rocked to and fro a few more times, trying to decide how to handle this new situation.

At last, he sat down, but as he did, he kept repeating, "This is my spot, my spot, my spot, my spot."

Bill waited as Chief seated himself.

Chief continued to babble about this was his spot, repeating it over and over until Bill finally said, "OK, enough already!" Chief stopped, opened his coffee carefully then lit a cigarette. As he put the pack of smokes back in his shirt pocket, he looked over at the stranger, wondering what this interloper wanted. The fear of the unknown was a phobia of Chief's. Also, he didn't like it when people pushed themselves on him. This stranger was no different and he wished he'd leave. He slipped in a "This is my spot" under his breath.

"Will you teach me how to work a corner?" Bill finally asked, looking as Chief smoked and drank his coffee.

He then proceeded to tell Chief how he had had a bad run of luck. His wife had divorced him, had taken him to court and basically got the house and most of the assets.

"Truth is she had a better lawyer than I was," he admitted. He didn't tell Chief about the other woman, or he how he like to drink. Or, and how he lost his position.

In a divorce there are three truths: the wife's truth; the husband's truth; and, the actual truth. In this case the actual truth equated to Bill was a boozer, womanizer, and a lousy lawyer.

He admitted he lost his position with a Seattle law firm, lost his family which included his wife, children, and a nice house in the suburbs.

Further, he confessed that after a few more nights of drinking, womanizing, and feeling sorry for himself, he moved to Yakima, rented a motel room by the month, looked for a job, ran out of unemployment, and was on the verge of being evicted.

He related how on a recent day, when taking the bus to interview for a job, he saw Chief on the corner, panhandling. Asking other passengers on the bus, they told him the panhandler was called Chief Kamiakin and he worked the same corner almost every day.

Bill had thought to himself, "This guy must be making money or he wouldn't keep doing it." After getting turned down for another job he decided to meet the Chief.

"I need to meet this guy," he had said quietly to himself and today he made it happen.

"People tell me you're called Chief Kamiakin," Bill disclosed to Chief. "They say you've been working the same corner for as long as they can remember. If that's true, then, you must be making money."

Chief took a drag on his cigarette, blew the smoke out then took a sip of coffee. He looked straight ahead, not directly at Bill.

Finally he said, "Call me Chief. It's not my name, but everyone calls me it. It's not my name, not my name." He looked around the immediate area, but avoided looking at Bill, and gave a lamented sigh, adding "This is my spot."

The cigarette smoke poured from his mouth as he said this, then, added, "OK, call me Chief, it's not my name, but you can call me Chief. Everyone calls me Chief." Hurriedly he threw in, "It's not my name, not my name, not my name."

Both men were then silent for a few minutes, both were uneasy; but nonetheless, both were determined to remain faithful to their own needs. Neither was willing to allow the other any room for comfort, each caught up in their own self-interest.

"Chief, I know this is your spot," the stranger conceded, "but I need your help. I need to learn how to work a corner.

"Corner?" Chief questioned apprehensively, then, asked, "What corner?" As he thought about it he grew confused and agitated. "Corner? My corner?" he queried. His agitation grew.

Suddenly he stood-up, threw away his coffee cup and looked directly at Bill, the stranger, "You can't have my corner! No! No! No!" Chief began to shift his weight back and forth, from one foot to the other, then, back again. Faster and faster he rocked, shouting, "No, no, it's my corner."

Bill was staggered by what he was witnessing and didn't quite know what to do. He watched as Chief became more and more frantic. "What is this?" he thought to himself. At last, he decided Chief was "short a full load of bricks" and he, Bill, needed to get control of the situation.

"Chief, settle down," he commanded, "settle down, I don't want your corner." He repeated, "I don't want your corner." He watched as his words seemed to have a calming effect. He repeated again that he didn't want Chief's corner. After reiterating the message of not wanting Chief's corner, Chief start to relax and calm down.

Suddenly, Chief looked at his watch. He looked up at Bill and said, "Time to go back. It's my corner. This is my spot."

As he turned to go he looked over his shoulder, stopped for a moment then signaled with a wave of his hand for Bill to follow him.

It made no sense to Bill, but he grabbed his stuff and hurried to catch up with Chief. As he did, Chief said, "I'll help, but it's my corner, my corner, my corner."

So that day, for the first time, people driving to work, passed by two panhandlers. The one they knew as Chief was standing in front of another panhandler whose sign read, "My Wife Had A Better Lawyer, please help."

Chief coached over his shoulder to Bill, "Look at the sidewalk! Hold your sign under your chin but on top of your whiskers. Watch me! Pay attention!" Several times he was also heard to say to his protégé, "This is my corner." Then, after a time, they would work the corner without a word exchanged between them.

Back and forth it went. Sometimes Bill would be in front. Sometimes Chief would lead. When a donation was imminent, whoever was in front would retrieve the money and quickly slip it into his pocket, then, take-up the second position.

For weeks, the unlikely pair worked the corner. They showed-up every business work day with Chief helping Bill to learn the ways of panhandling. Bill was surprised to find he actually made good money, not great money, but enough to pay the rent for his small motel room, buy some food, and have enough left for smokes, a few beers, and pool. Chief came to accept Bill, but as more time passed, he never failed to remind Bill, "It's my corner." Bill was a good student and learned quickly. He came to appreciate Chief's situation. He learned to tolerate the autism that afflicted his mentor.

It was during one of their midday lunch breaks that Bill announced to Chief he appreciated everything Chief had taught him, but the time had come for him to move to another corner.

Chief looked questioningly at him, then, said, "But this is our corner, our corner, our corner?"

"No," Bill answered. "This is your corner. I need to give it back to you. It's yours and I need to move on."

Chief looked at Bill with a blank, uncomprehending stare. "Will you go?" he finally asked.

And the day came that Bill established himself a few blocks east of the corner he had shared with Chief.

The corner of Fair Avenue and Nob Hill was almost as busy as their old shared corner. People were almost as generous as those at Nob Hill and First. The paradox was that Bill made more money for himself at his new corner.

It was turning out to be a great corner for Bill, except, for the bar situated just a half block away. It had a pool table, a sport that Bill loved to play, in which he was skilled, but never overpowering. The bar and the pool table drew Bill like a strong magnet bending electricity and as time passed, Bill frequented the El Rey more often than he did his corner.

It was also during this period of time that an event took place that would have a major impact on the city of Yakima, including upon Chief and Bill directly.

In the beginning, there didn't seem to be any connection between the actions of the city council and the lives of the two panhandlers.

Because the city council decided to build a new jail to house more prisoners from King County (which had an overcrowding issue according to a court ruling), the City of Yakima and the lives of the two corner warriors would be inescapably affected.

The city council, looking at their budget, suddenly realized their city's coffers were becoming depleted due to the high crime and gang issues now prevalent amongst the city. Over eighty percent of the city's annual budget was being used for law enforcement and the prosecution of criminals. This was an enormous drain on the city, plus it made the city council look like they couldn't deal with anything but crime.

As the city fathers looked around for a solution, they discovered a federal grant was being offered to cities that were willing to build jail facilities. The cost to the city would be nothing at best, and at worst, minimal.

Some months prior to this development, Yakima's city manager had received a letter from King County asking what the city's interest might be in renting excess jail space to King County to house some of their over-crowded prison population. King County would pay for shipping the prisoners to Yakima and then pay a daily stipend to house each prisoner for the remainder of his incarceration.

The Yakima City Council members took one look at this and realized how much money was at stake. They reasoned if they were able to house seventy prisoners a day at a profit of twenty-five dollars each, the profit to the city coffers would be enormous—almost two thousand dollars a day.

It was a win-win situation. The effect on the budget would be a gain of over a half million dollars a year. What city councilman could pass up such an opportunity? Actually, two members of council did see problems with such a scheme, and they said so.

The discussion went on for several meetings with study sessions, community comment time, and local organizations issuing their take on the situation. During the time of this debate, Chief and Bill continued working their respective corners.

Chief's routine remained unaltered but Bill was slowly sinking back to drinking too much and losing his panhandling money to pool sharks. Many mornings his corner stood empty while he went to the bar to have an early morning "pick-me-up" and try to win back some of his money.

Then one fine spring day at the city council meeting, one of the members announced the Federal grant being offered would allow Yakima to build a new jail housing no less than one hundred fifty prisoners. As the member was announcing this amazing windfall and the money it would generate for the city, Bill was losing his small motel room over on Fruitvale Blvd due to his lack of rent money.

Up on his corner, Chief had just collected a twenty. The city council voted to apply for the grant, which they subsequently won with ease. While accepting bids for the construction of the new jail, the council signed a five year contract with King County to house up to one hundred prisoners a day at a price which gave a healthy daily profit to the city's treasury.

"My God man, how could one go wrong?" exclaimed a long-time councilman. He, and the rest of the council, overlooked the attached clause about the release of prisoners back into society.

That clause stated that a prisoner, having served his time, could be released on his own recognizance anywhere he chose. Most prisoners elected to stay in Yakima and try to start over.

They elected to remain in the city because the release money was minimal at best and none had a job waiting back in King County. So they stayed and most slipped back into their old, wicked ways.

Because of this, Yakima's population acquired a disproportionate amount of released sex offenders and arsonists. This loophole also caused a startling increase in criminal incidents such as burglary, gang activity, and just plain mean thieves who would rob people at gunpoint and then often pistol-whip their victims. Home invasions increased at an alarming rate, too.

It was during this time of jail building and the housing of offenders that Bill was increasing his time at the El Rey.

In the early morning hours, he would find his way to his corner at Sixth and Nob Hill to panhandle just long enough to get a stash of dollar bills with which to fund his gambling and drinking for the day. By ten o'clock, he would high-tail it to the El Rey where a beer awaited him. When he arrived, if no one was at the pool table, he would sit at the bar with a beer and cigarette.

In the time it took to drink a beer, usually someone showed an interest in getting a game of pool going.

This particular morning two young guys showed up together, each ordered a beer and five-dollars in quarters to use at the pool table. Bill sat there with his back to the pool table, drinking his beer but following everything underway at the table.

"Eight ball, Fred?" the short, stocky one asked his partner.

"Hell, yes," the taller one declared as he took a swig of his beer. Then he added, "Ahhh, fuck'n good beer. It's good to be out, ain't it?"

His companion nodded in agreement as he gathered the pool balls into the rack and positioned them for his partner to break and start the game.

There was a pause as Fred lined up his breaking shot, then, WHACK, and the balls split apart and the game was on. A shiver went through Bill as he turned to watch the game's progress.

While these events were happening, Chief was out on his corner, his sign out, a contrite smile on his face as he looked down at the sidewalk. He slowly paced against the traffic.

It was a bright, warm day, one of those special days when people felt like giving. By ten o'clock, Chief had fifty bucks in his special pocket. Internally, he was beaming with success, but he remained careful not to show it to his donors.

At the El Rey, the two ex-cons shooting pool had invited Bill to put a quarter on the rail. This meant he would play the winner of the present game.

Bill sat at the bar while Fred and his partner finished their game; all the while he was deciding how he would play this one.

As the match progressed, the two friends chided each other and teased, if one missed an easy shot. Both were generally good humored and seemed eager to enjoy the match.

Fred's friend, while waiting for Fred to shoot, walked over to his brew, looked at Bill and asked, "What's your name? I'm called Lefty." He picked up his beer as he waited for Bill to answer.

"I'm Bill," as he reached out to shake Lefty's hand. At that moment, Fred yelled, "Bullshit! How'd I miss such an easy shot?"

Without shaking Bill's hand, Lefty turned to the table laughing. Bill watched Lefty line up a corner shot which any novice could make. Fred stood next to Bill taking a couple gulps of his beer, then, suddenly said jauntily to Lefty, "Don't miss asshole."

As he and Bill watch, Lefty tapped the white cue ball, missing the easy shot. Bill couldn't help snickering to himself as Fred yelled and made fun of Lefty's misfortune.

"Got your ass now, Sucker," he chided Lefty. "Get your dollar out, it's mine."

"You ain't made the eight-ball yet," he called back to Fred.

Fred was lining up the eight-ball for a side pocket as Lefty was pulling a stack of bills out of the front of his Levi pocket.

Bill's eyes widened a bit as he looked at the wad over his glass while taking a long swig of beer.

"Looks like he's got you Lefty," Bill stated flippantly to Lefty as he got ready for his turn. He turned to the barkeep and asked for quarters, thinking to himself this is going to be a long, but profitable afternoon.

For the next three hours the three men played game after game, each trying to get an edge over the other two, each trying to figure out the skill level of his opponent, and each probing the other for weaknesses.

Bill was careful to win only a few games. He mostly sat watching the two friends bantering and joking with each other. During this time, the trio exchanged stories about each other's lives. Fred was very interested in Bill's panhandling career.

Bill explained how he had been down on his luck when he saw Chief at the corner of Nob Hill and First Street. "So, I looked him up one day," Bill exulted, "asked him to teach me how to do it?" He waited for moment, then, added, "He did good by me."

Fred was watching Lefty take his shot. He asked, "Can you make any money standing there all day? Seems like lot 'a work, does it pay?"

"It's not a lot," Bill answered. "I never did like Chief. He's real good. Somethin' about how he works the drivers," Pausing a moment, then added, "Never completely figured it out."

Fred was looking at Lefty when he said, "So, it's Chief that makes the big money." A look of understanding passed between the two as Lefty threw his pool cue down because he had lost the game by putting the eight-ball accidently into a corner pocket. "Piss," was his only comment!

Bill had been watching the two friends closely. He was trying to decide if these two had a scam going, or if they were just two regular guys out for a fun morning. Neither, it seemed, to shoot very good pool, which Bill appreciated.

Bill considered himself a hustler and as a hustler he hadn't shot his best that morning. He was trying to decide which one would be his mark. Now he figured Lefty was not worth bothering with except to use him as cover while he set up Fred. Lefty had just lost again, and it was a good time to start working Fred.

As Bill stepped to the table, he inserted his quarter to drop the balls for Fred to rack, and asked Fred, "Hey, want to put something more on this game, pal?"

Fred looked at him, "Sure, what'cha have in mind?"

As Bill nodded, he laid a five on the table which Bill matched.

Fred walked to the end of the table to watch Bill break, he looked at Lefty knowingly while saying to Bill, "Tell us more about this Chief."

* * * * *

The day had been hot and bright with the traffic heavy. Chief had been working his corner all day and as the sun was settling into the Western sky he was thinking it was time to call it a day. He reached down to his right pocket with his right hand and felt the wad of bills.

He thought he could quit a bit early today because he knew the amount he had taken in was high, higher perhaps than his best day last year when he collected over a one hundred eight dollars. Maybe today he had accumulated more. He was excited.

Suddenly, he remembered. When the present light turned green, he turned away from the traffic, bent over and with his left hand checked his left shoestrings to make sure they were tied properly. At the same time he checked his left sock, which was a high-top sock, to make sure his morning collection was still secure. Every day at lunch he would roll up his morning's collections. Using a large rubber band, he would secure the money to his left shin, then he covered it with his high-top sock. Today he was pleased to note this roll felt big, too.

"That's it," he thought to himself. Instead of turning back to the traffic, he collected his plastic grocery bag and headed towards McDonald's and his place behind the trash can.

"Thinking, I'll get me a coffee to drink," he thought jovially.

When he reached the McDonald's parking lot, he joyfully exclaimed, "What a day, a day, a day!" He caught himself and returned to his quiet demeanor.

At the counter, a server who knew him asked, "What'cha have, Chief?"

"A coffee, cheese burger and fries," Chief answered gleefully. As the server took his money, she couldn't help notice how happy he was acting. She commented, "Wow, Chief, you must'a had a good day?"

Chief smiled an absent smile, paid his money as she set his order on the counter. She took his money, which was exact, and Chief took his food and drink.

Neither paid attention to the two young men standing away from the counter. When Chief left with his order, the taller one stepped up to the counter and asked the server, "Is that Chief?"

"Sure is," she innocently replied, turning to make a new pot of coffee. She didn't give a second thought to the two scruffy men who following Chief out the side door.

Chief had just settled-in to drink his coffee and eat his cheeseburger when a stranger appeared around a corner of the large trash bin.
He stood there a moment, then asked, "You, Chief?"

Chief, who had just sat down, automatically said, "This is my spot." He un-wrapped the cheeseburger and as he took a bite of it, another stranger came around the other corner of the trash container.

Chief quickly realized he was penned in. This unnerved Chief and he swallowed his mouthful quickly, repeating, "This is my spot, my spot, my spot."

The first stranger said, "Chief, we just want to talk with you." He took a slow, ominous step towards Chief as the other stranger also came in closer to Chief. "My name's Fred," the stranger added. "I, we need your help," as he pointed to the other stranger.

"No," Chief said, his voice full of fear. "This is my spot, my spot. You go away." He stood up, spilling his coffee, dropping his burger.

Quickly he grabbed his grocery bag quickly started to leave, but Fred stepped in front of him and demanded, "Stop, damn it!"

Chief stopped, looked behind to the other stranger who was moving towards him also. "What you want, you want?" he asked weakly.

Fred looked at his partner, Lefty, then, said to Chief, "We need some money. Your friend Bill said you would help."

With anxiety and fright, Chief looked at Lefty not sure what he was hearing from Fred. "Bill?" he questioned as he looked back at Fred. "Bill, who? My frw'end Bill?"

"The guy you taught to panhandle," Fred answered irritated, his eyes narrowing. "We talked to him this morning. He told us you were good at this begging stuff."

"Don't know no Bill," Chief quivered, his lower lip trembled.

"Sure you do, asshole," Lefty said almost in Chief's ear. Lefty's voice had a hard edge when he added, "We know you know him."

Chief looked around Fred for a means of escape, then placed his back against the trash receptacle and looked behind Lefty. He repeated, "This is my spot, my spot, my spot." He said it over and over as the two strangers hemmed him in.

Then he bolted towards Lefty, the shorter of the two, but Lefty grabbed him around the throat, and practically lifted him off the ground.

"Fred, I'm getting tired of this B.S.," he said to his partner as he lifted Chief. He looked at Chief and demanded, "Where's your fuckin' money?"

Chief quaked, "Haven't got no money." As he said it, he reached his right hand down to his pocket to make sure his money was still there.

Fred warily cautioned his partner, "Lefty, cool down, Bro."

"My ass," Lefty responded pulling out a six-inch switchblade. "I'll knife this asshole!" He looked at Chief with murder and desperation all rolled into one wicked glare.

"You better give him the money," Fred said looking Chief in the eyes. "Chief, the man's dangerous."

"I don't have no money," Chief cried, tears streaming down his cheeks, as he clutched his right pocket full of his morning donations. He thought of the hours on the corner, what a great day it had been, and the amount of donations he collected; now, all for naught.

Lefty plunged the knife into Chief's side, blood spurted out, and Chief cried out, "Please, no, don't, HELP!" His day went black as he slumped to the pavement. Someone on the other side of the trash receptacle yelled, "Call the cops!"

Fred, hearing someone yell for the cops, turned the slumping body of Chief's over and pulled the money out of his right pocket. Lefty was looking through Chief's grocery bag as second stranger came around the side of the trash bin.

He turned to Fred, indicating to go, but he tripped over Chief's limp body when he noticed the bulge in Chief's left sock. With a single swipe of his switchblade, he cut open the sock along with Chief's leg. The roll of money fell to the ground as blood spouted from the wound. Fred grabbed the roll as he and Lefty fled the scene.

More people were coming over to the trash bin, but the two thieves ran past them before anyone realized who they were and what had happened.

* * * * *

Thanks to the quick actions of the people in the McDonald's parking lot, the speed of the Yakima police getting to the scene, and the skill of the paramedics, Chief Kamiakin survived the robbery.

The police were able to piece together what had happened, and more importantly, who was responsible.

Earlier that afternoon the police had been called to the El Rey Bar where they had found a victim out behind the bar, unconscious, and with knife wounds. While the victim never talked to the police, the bartender was able to describe to the police what had happened. He said the victim was one of three men who had come in early that morning and started shooting pool and drinking beer. Two of the men were strangers to the barkeep, but the victim was a regular named Bill. "I think the two strangers had recently been released from jail," the barkeep had stated.

Further, he also was able to give the police a description of the two men. He said he knew the taller man was called Fred and the shorter one was Lefty. A detective showed the bartender some mug shots, and the two men he recognized were identified as recent parolees from the new jail.

When asked what happened between the men, the bartender said he knew Bill was a hustler and that he was trying to hustle the two men. The game went on until about one o'clock in the afternoon. By then, Bill had won a lot of money. The taller man, Fred, seemed all right with everything, but the shorter man, Lefty, was upset. The bartender heard him tell his partner that he was going to get his money back from Bill.

Around two o'clock, Bill left through the backdoor, at least, that's what the bartender thought had happened. Next thing he knew Lefty came running in and told Fred they needed to go, fast.

As they were leaving Fred asked his partner if they had time to look up someone named "Chief" up at Nob Hill and First. Lefty said, "Hell yes," and they hightailed out of the bar.

"I got suspicious," the bartender proudly said. He related how he went out the backdoor and found Bill lay bleeding against the back wall of the bar.

"That's when I called 911," he finished. "I tried to stop the bleeding, but not much luck," he concluded, adding, "Got to get inside, we're getting busy."

* * * * *

When Chief became conscious, he looked around the room trying to understand what happened. The room was dim with the blinds closed and there was another bed in the room. Up on the wall was a television showing a movie but no sound. Next to his bed was a tray with a glass of water and a pitcher. There was another tray of the same type at the other side of the second bed.

Suddenly, Chief became scared and starting yelling, "This isn't my spot, not my spot, not my spot! Where am I?" He was frantic with fear, then, looking under the covers he discovered his own clothes were not on him.

"What is this?" he asked the person in the other bed. "Where are we?"

The other person made no move to answer his questions. Chief looked closely as he tried to turn on his side but discovered he was in a safety harness and could hardly move.

"Hey, you!" he yelled at his roommate, but the roommate didn't answer. Suddenly, the door to the room opened and two large women dressed as nurses came into the room.

"Chief, you alright?" the first nurse asked while the second nurse went to the other bed. Before Chief could answer, the second nurse called for a Code Blue. "Christ, Emily, this one isn't breathing," the second nurse said to the nurse standing by Chief's bed.

Within a few minutes, doctors and nurses of all sizes and shapes came rushing to the hospital room, over to the second bed by the window. Chief was hysteria wrapped in panic.

"This isn't my space," Chief again started yelling. "I have to go. Let me up. I have to go, I have to go. This isn't my space." He looked around in sheer panic. Sweat was collecting on his brow as he pulled up his bed sheets to hide under.

The first nurse, a large black lady, told Chief he was going to need to calm down, that everything and everyone will be safe.

"Honey," she said in a husky voice, "You're going to be fine. So will your roommate. His name is Bill."

As the Code Blue team worked on Bill, Chief remembered he knew a Bill. "Bill, Bill, Bill?" he repeated several times. He looked across at the person in the second bed. Looking at his nurse, he stammered, "That's not Bill, not Bill, not Bill."

He looked again, then, laid back down in his bed. He said loudly, "This isn't my space. I want to go, NOW!" He paused, but got no reaction. "I want to go now, this isn't my space," he whimpered.

"Honey, you gotta stay here. You're hurt," the big nurse said as she straightened out his bed sheets. "Let's let go of the sheets," she commanded easily. She watched him a moment as he calmed down as the Blue Team was leaving.

The other nurse she said she didn't know why admission hadn't put this one in the psych ward. "That's not Bill," she heard him whisper again and again.

"I don't either," said the other nurse, "but somehow these two are connected." She stopped and looked at Chief, then, said, "Oh Hell, Honey, he's the guy you see over at Nob and First beggin fer money." Now she double checked her patient, adjusted his drip line and suggested to her work-mate, "Let's go take our break."

When the two nurses were gone, Chief looked over at his roommate, but the roommate was asleep.

"That's not Bill," Chief thought, not realizing he said it audibly.

Suddenly, the door of the room opened and a young nurse with a syringe came through the door. She walked up to Chief's bed and greeted him with a big smile.

"You Chief?" she asked as she took hold of his wrist to look at his ID bracelet.

Chief tried to pull away but the nurse held his wrist tightly as she read his name. "Yep, you're the one," she said, then, commanded, "Turn over on your side."

"Why?" Chief stammered and stuttered, then yelled, "This isn't my space! I'm going now! I'm going now!" However, he was restrained with the waistband that tied him to the bed.

"This is going to be easy," the nurse thought to herself. "Come on Chief, turn a bit," the pretty nursed coaxed.

As Chief turned on one side, she quickly lifted his hospital gown and administered the shot.

"You hurt me, you hurt me!" he cried out.

"I didn't hurt you." she quipped.

He looked at the nurse with tear filled eyes and sobbed, "This isn't my space, not my space." Soon he was asleep as the shot took effect.

Later in the same afternoon, Chief woke, looked around apprehensively, and in a frightened tone asked, "Where am I, this isn't my space." Someone in the next bed moved.

"You're right," the person said in a pained voice. He carefully shifted his weight so he could lie on his side and look across at Chief.

Around his head were bandages, one eye was covered, and his other eye was puffy and black. "That you, Chief?" the person asked.

Chief looked at the person in the opposite bed, but it scared him because the person looked so frightful. He looked away, then, back again. At last he said, "This isn't my space."

"Yes, I know," the unsightly person answered. "Chief, it's me, Bill." He waited, but when Chief failed to respond he went on, "I got jumped by two guys that beat me up."

He looked at Chief, knowing Chief was having a hard time understanding what had happened, and that he was Bill. "Chief, it's me, Bill," he repeated.

Chief raised his head a bit and looked at him. He looked again, then studied him but failed to recognize him. "This isn't my space," he said again. He was like a child refusing to acknowledge reality. This other person was hideous, and he wanted no part of him. He only wanted to go home.

"Chief, it's me, Bill," Bill tried again. He waited but nothing. Then Bill said, "You taught me how to panhandle on your corner."

Chief stopped repeating himself and looked over at Bill. He studied Bill for minutes before saying, "Bill, My friend, Bill? Something familiar clicked. Chief began to understand the person in the next bed was someone from his past. He was still cautious, but judiciously came to conclude it was someone within his world.

"What I teach you?" he asked carefully.

"Chief, you taught me how to work your corner," Bill replied. "You taught me how to hold my sign, what to do when people gave me money. How to walk. You taught me how to survive."

"I did?" Chief hesitated.

Bill, in a raspy voice, resolved, "Yes, you did. You saved me in so many ways, Chief."

"Then," Chief paused, then, posed, "Why did you hurt me?" He began to cry and tremble, he asked again, "Why did you hurt me?"

As Chief sobbed, Bill said, "I didn't hurt you. I just opened my big mouth too much. I'm sorry."

He explained to Chief how he had started drinking too much again, shooting too much pool, and hustling guys. While Chief listened quietly, Bill confessed how he told the two criminals all about how you had trained me and how good you were at getting donations.

"Guess I shouldn't told them that," Bill finished, then, added, "Chief, I'm sorry."

Chief laid there for a long time after Bill finished, seemingly in deep thought. He was trying desperately to comprehend all that had happened to him, and now this person from his past was confessing to lapses and mistakes.

Finally, Chief had his conclusions and in a childlike, lyrical voice stated, "I have a question?"

"Anything," Bill replied. "Anything"

Chief braced himself up on his left elbow and looked around the room, studying it for several minutes. He, then, looked at Bill and innocently asked, "Is this your space?"

Afternoon Tea

The heralds of spring trumpeted through the cold, damp soil, their blooms barely above the earth. Each blossom reaching skyward, each blossom displaying its own brilliance, and each blossom's yellow pistils heavy with fertile, powdery dew waiting a breezy fulfillment. Rich in color, strong in character, the little flowers were clustered together, planted by caring hands, trumpeting to all who would listen that change was about. The seasons change ever so slowly—ever so relentlessly.

Beth was in her kitchen washing the few dishes of her singular breakfast. The paper lay unopened on the dining table; a spot of coffee marred its headline. "*Super Tuesday Show Down*," read the caption. Bush was due to edge McCain, Gore to destroy Bradley. Beth had not noticed and did not care. Today was her day!

"Oh, yes," thought Beth. Her youthful vitality belied her sixty-eight years. One could tell that she had been an athletic person, especially skilled at running, her movements displaying the grace of a past champion. And to her way of thinking, no one could beat her, ever. She did win the final race from cross-town rival, Eastside High, she thought to herself.

"So long ago," she sighed as she viewed the new Crocus blooms through her kitchen window. "Today will be wonderful," she remarked to herself, thinking of how fleeting victory really is.

She busied herself planning the menu. It must be perfect. Some Girl Scout cookies, a small Marie Calendar pie, peach. Did she need to consider ice cream, its costly?

"No, the girls wouldn't appreciate ice cream," she said aloud. "They'd have fifty reasons why they couldn't eat ice cream. All medical," she sighed. The doctor said this, and the doctor said that as she thought of their past conversations.

"Dr. McJefferies' nurse told me in confidence that the doctor doesn't like his patients to fill up on ice cream, but that he eats more than anyone should," Old Margaret would tell someone in confidence, almost yelling in their ear. Margaret deals in strictly QT stuff.

"What else should I serve," Beth asked herself, apprehensively. She had been standing at the counter of her kitchen thinking about all this when the phone rang.

"Hello," she answered almost too loudly. A voice at the other end asked how she was doing.

"Who is this," Beth asked!

"Mother," the voice said. "It's your daughter, Peggy!"

"Peggy?"

"Yes, Peggy," Beth's daughter replied! "Good God, mother, are you all right?"

"Peggy, listen, I'm real busy right now! Having some friends in for tea this afternoon," Beth explained. It never occurred to her that Peggy might not need anything. That maybe she just wanted to visit.

"I take it you can't baby sit, then," Peggy teased?

"Today, you mean today," was her mom's reply? "Can't, not today! I'm getting ready for the afternoon tea."

"Dad said to say hello," her daughter interjected. "We went to lunch last Thursday and ate at The Counter in the Pioneer Square Mall."

Beth thought about this a moment. She was glad that Peggy and her dad could get together and talk occasionally. Then Beth replied, "Is he O.K.?" Tom never asked about her before, not for the last five years anyway. Then she thought, my God, its five years since he left me.

Earlier that morning, as she rose out of bed, she had noticed herself in the closet mirror. Her frame was slight, not bony nor heavy. Firm came to mind. Her skin was firm for her age; she would be sixty-nine at her next birthday. "This next June," she had thought.

Peggy would give her the usual birthday party and everyone would make a fuss over how good she looked, that she had not aged a bit since they met her.

Beth appeared young for her age, her short hair curled tight against her head, the bangs covering half her forehead. She never went out without making sure her hair was in perfect order.

"To think, Tom left her for someone younger, some fifty-eight old," she said to herself in the mirror. "Well, I don't look so bad myself," as she turned from the mirror and headed down to the kitchen.

She had moved into the Indian Hills Condominiums four years ago. The condominium was so damn small that at first she felt it was closing in on her from all sides. It took her six months to adjust to the unusually minuscule size of this crackerjack box. Nevertheless, it would have to do because it fit the budget, no thanks to Tom.

"The creep," she thought aloud while trying to find tea in the pantry.

Her husband, Tom, had divorce her suddenly. In fact, it happened so fast that she gave him about everything he wanted without thinking-the home, the newer car, most of the bank accounts, everything, just everything. She did not think to ask for support.

Now she was stuck in this undersized, crackerjack condominium that didn't have enough room to even have one guest let alone five. Moreover, she had to work hard to make enough money to pay for everything. Men really do fair better in divorce than women, or so they say.

"Who's they?" she thought to herself.

"So, you and Daddy had lunch together," She asked Peggy questioningly, returning to the present? "Was he alone?"

"Yes, Mom, he was alone," was Peggy's smug reply. "I think he might be having trouble keeping up with Dorothy. She's a handful."

"Well, he is seventy-eight," Beth stated. Serves him right she thought to herself. Her eyes narrowed wickedly for a second as she thought of Tom succumbing to a heart attack in the middle of a Viagra induced moment. Then the corner of her mouth curled up a bit and her eyes twinkled.

"Listen, Honey, I have five women from the Condo complex coming over for tea this afternoon. We've formed a Hospice volunteer group and I need to get going if you have nothing important to tell me," she explained. "I want this tea to go perfectly. It's my first one."

"Oh, Mom, I know you and it will go off without a hitch. Do you need anything?" Peggy asked. "I'm going to Safeway, if you need anything and I can drop it off?"

"No, I'm good," Beth replied. She thought for a moment as Peggy and she said good-by. No, she wasn't forgetting anything.

"Love you, Mom," Said Peggy warmly. Beth returned the love and hung-up.

* * * * * *

The morning and early afternoon went quickly and the grandfather clock was striking three o'clock. Beth had just completed setting the cookies and cake on the small coffee table situated in the living room. She had changed into a nice blue poke-a-dotted dress with a lace collar. She step back to look at the perfectly set coffee table with the teacups gathered at one end, along with the sugar, creamer and Nutria-sweet.

Margaret would insist on Nutria-sweet. Everything was in ready and she knew she needed to hurry because food-loving Gloria would be first – Gloria was always first.

Beth flew up the stairs and was just finishing her makeup when she heard the doorbell ring. "Good timing," she said aloud.

"Afternoon, Gloria," Beth greeted Gloria. "What's in the box?"

"Cookies, from the panaderia," replied Gloria with a twinge of accent. "The bakery," she explained to Beth. "Oh, the coffee table looks great. What are these …," she asked as she picked up one of the Girl Scout cookies to try. "Hmmm," She said with a full mouth. "I just love food."

"We know, Gloria," Beth replied with a wispy smile.

She heard the doorbell rang again and walked over to open the door. Standing there talking was Mary, Nadyne and Ruth. Behind them came Margaret, slowly, using her walker.

Margaret was 92 years old, hard of hearing and near-sighted. She had been married five times, four times since she was 60, had owned a bar in which she found all four of the later husbands. She always said they were all pickled when she married them but they all had money and she needed that to keep the bar open. Her few customers loved her and came often for food, drink and conversation.

Margaret loved to tell everyone how she was born right alongside the Snake River and, even, she had once met the author, John Steinbeck. Evenings at the Tav were warm, fun and always memorable. Margaret didn't retire until she was 88 and then her grandson had to push hard.

Mary stepped through the door first and gave Beth a hug. Looking around the living room, she told Beth how nice the room looked and then spotted Gloria in the kitchen getting a plate for her Mexican cookies.

Mary and Gloria had worked together as paraprofessionals in the local middle school. While Gloria irritated Mary with her endless talk about food, they still remained good friends and Mary worried about her like a mother would worry about her overweight daughter.

"What have you got," Mary asked mischievously, a twinkle in her eye?

Gloria looked up with guilt and replied, "Cookies from the panaderia. Want one?" Mary watched as Gloria came around the counter with the plate of cookies and she noticed the half-eaten one in Gloria's hand, which Gloria was coyly trying to hide.

Ruth's high-pitched voice interjected saying, "She's hiding a cookie." She walked up to Gloria and said, "Dear, you're eating way too many cookies. Look at you, oh dear!"

Gloria, totally embarrassed, gave Ruth a look that was one of hurt and wanted to give her a good swat on the ass. But, she liked Ruth and always enjoyed her views on life, husbands and sex.

Ruth thought she was the sex expert, even at an age when most women had dismissed it as an irritation. She would be seventy her next birthday but she still talked about sex with anyone who would listen, giving them the dos and don'ts. Her hair was dyed a red brunette color with high lights of blonde, she said that the highlights are what attracted the men.

"Ruth, you're the one who said that men like big handles they can grab." Gloria expressed through her embarrassment. She walked out of the kitchen area before Ruth could reply.

"Hi, Mary," Gloria quickly said dismissing Ruth, nodding at Mary and then looked around the room for a place to sit. There was a place next to Margaret on the couch and she plopped down heavily.

"You're not going to get a husband if you keep eating those," said Margaret as Ruth took a bite of a cookie.

Margaret gave a knowing look at Mary hoping for some support but Mary just smiled and then turned to speak, telling Beth how nice everything looked.

Nadyne, as usual looked at everything as if it was beneath her level of expectation. The colors were not right, why would you mix types of furniture and those lamps.

"Where did you get these lamps," she asked almost knowing they had come from TJ Maxx. She looked for a price tag but found none but did find a couple of scratches that made the lamps sure candidates for Maxx inventory. Why do you shop there Beth, she thought to herself.

"Oh, those, they came from Ross," Beth replied, knowing Nadyne was probably having a cow over her buying them on the cheap.

Nadyne just nodded smugly.

Everyone had served themselves tea and cookies or cake except for Ruth who had one of everything. Well, she is enjoying herself thought Beth; I just hope everyone will leave her alone about her weight.

"Mary," Beth said aloud, "shall we get the meeting going?"

* * * * * *

Ruth in her high-pitched voice was saying, "People at those events won't buy a lot of raffle tickets. Beth, you're new and don't know these people like we do." Ruth looked around the group for support.

Margaret was just sitting there staring straight ahead. Mary had raised her hand and was waiting for Ruth to acknowledge her. Gloria was stuffing a cookie in her mouth and nodding agreement with Ruth.

"You should stick to going to the mall," Nadyne interjected. She was looking at the underside of the Beth's cookie plates with some contempt. Cheap china, she thought as she set the piece back down.

"Oh, Margaret," shrieked Ruth, "what do you think?"

Margaret just continued to sit, her eyes looking like two glistening saucers.

Gloria, sitting next to her, gave her a gentle tap on the forearm.

"My God," Gloria exclaimed. "Margaret, are you OK?" Gloria started to get up and take Margaret by the arm.

"Margaret, wakeup!" she yelled. "Oh, God! Beth, something is wrong with Margaret!"

Beth jumped up and went over to Margaret and shook her gently. "Mary, call 911. Hurry!"

By this time, everyone was standing around Margaret wondering what they should do. Mary made a dash for the phone and had the 911 operator on the line.

Later, after Margaret had been hauled off to the hospital and all the ladies had gone home, Beth's phone rang.

"Mom?" Beth's daughter said into the phone. "Mom, is everything OK? Was your tea a success?"

"Everything was a success," Beth answered. "But it ended with Margaret dying in my living room."

Peggy said simply, "I'll be right over."

Outside, the crocus blooms stood proudly, heralding the coming seasons, assuring all who would take note that the world would go on.

Beth looked out her window at the little flowers. This day the colors were richer, the blooms more defined and distinct. Her mood demurred but her faith in life was strengthened by the little flowers that always reached for the sun.

She met her daughter at the driveway as Peggy emerged from the car and hugged her warmly. "I'm glad you came," she said quietly.

A Sparrow's Song

He looks normal. Walking home from school, Brian Wells looks just like any other young teen. His height is normal, his size is normal, his dress is normal. Everything about him is normal.

His hair is a moderate length with a cowlick. The black head of hair juts out like a plastic whiskbroom and dances as he talks.

Brian's clothes are neat and clean, his favorite plaid shirt is tucked into his brown trousers, and his tennis shoes have the normal amount of scuffmarks that would indicate their wearer is fourteen.

Walking from the bus stop to his home is four blocks in length and takes a normal person just a few minutes. As Brian walks, he adjusts his empty backpack. He is busy looking around for someone who might need him. Like his backpack, his house is empty.

"Hi, Mr. Henson," Brian calls out in a loud voice. "What'cha doin', Mr. Henson?" Without waiting for an answer, he follows his question, "My Dad has an axe! If you need it, I can go get it for you."

"Hi, Brian," Mr. Henson waves, his straw-hat sitting back on his gray head. He looks down at the large root he is cutting, then says to Brian, "No, Brian I don't need an ax."

"I can get it for you real quick," Brian calls hopefully from the gate. "Can I help you?" He starts to open the gate but Mr. Henson says,

"Brian, you better go home and check-in before stopping to help."

Brian stops at the gate for a moment, guilefully answers, "Oh, my folks don't mind me helping you, Mr. Henson. Besides, they're not home."

As he says this, he sees Mrs. Henson coming out on to the porch. "Hi, Mrs. Henson," Brian gives a spirited wave. He quickly adds, "I'm going to help Mr. Henson."

Mrs. Henson, dressed in her housecoat, wearing an apron comes down the steps towards Brian. "Brian, it would probably be better if you don't bother Mr. Henson today. He's needs to hurry."

Brian stops, looks at the Hensons, then looks down the street towards his empty house.

"Yeah, I need to get home, anyway, and let Gunner out of his pen." As he sees the sigh of relief come across the Hensons faces, he quickly adds, "Gunner's been penned up all day, I need to let him out." Then he remembers aloud, "It's one of my chores."

He closes the gate with resignation. In a jaunty tone, he calls out that he knows he can help Mr. Henson tomorrow.

Back on the street, he walks carelessly out towards the middle where a car sounds its horn. Brian jumps back.

"Sorry," he yells and another spirited wave. "Don't you live at the end of the street?" By this time, the car has past him and is speeding up with the driver shaking his head.

Forty-Fourth Avenue is a street of white clapboard homes and center-block houses. Each house on the street has its own style with some having cement drives, others asphalt. Most of the yards are neat and well maintained.

Of course, as with every neighborhood, there is one that has fallen below the standard of maintenance for the area. This "one" is Brian's house. It's a house in need of paint, both inside and out. Most windows don't work. Some are caught half way closed, or open. The neighbors argue that point. It's a house full of "Honey, I'm busy right now, damn it. I'll get to it."

It's to this house Brian goes. He walks on to the property and there is a decided change in his walk; a change of not being glad or happy about being home, more of a slide into resignation, a depression of sorts.

He throws his backpack onto the porch and watches it land in a broken Adirondack chair. It has a broken arm and a chewed leg. It has been needing paint for years. Like the rest of the house, it cries out for attention.

Dad will get that chair fixed soon, Brian thinks, then, he remembers Gunner. Aloud, he calls, "Com'n Gunner! Hold on boy!" He jumps off the porch, over the weed-filled roses, and starts to the backyard then stops.

"Hey, What'cha doin to your garden, Mrs. Jagger," Brian asks loudly? He goes to the waist-high gray cedar fence that divides his yard from Mrs. Jagger's cement drive. Before she can answer, Brian volunteers, "I can help you. Are you weeding? My Dad has a hoe. Want me to bring it?"

Mrs. Jagger, a sixth grade teacher, who is playing hooky for the day, looks up from her gardening and smiles.

"Brian, slow down." She straightens up and adjusts her hat. The hat has an oversized bill and completely shades her face. Her dark, deep-set eyes look at Brian and her wide smile is full of white teeth, behind red lips.

"Are you just getting home from school?" She asks.

"Yes, ma'am," Brian answers, while trying to remember where he put the hoe. "My Dad's hoe is real nice, ya' know," he quickly adds. "Dad buys only the best." He then follows quickly with, "He says that you should always buy good stuff. That it will last longer. Can I come help you?"

He doesn't wait for an answer before leaping over the short fence. "Dad put in this fence, ya' know."

Mrs. Jagger watches Brian as he walks across the driveway and comes through her neat, white picketed fence gate, a fence that runs between her garden and the driveway. She likes to works in the garden daily.

"Why don't you help me pick up these trimmings," she finally says as Brian joins her. "We don't need the hoe."

"My Dad always uses a hoe," Brian states. "I can find it, if you think we'll need it." Quickly, he adds, "It's in the shed. I know it's in the shed."

Stooping over the pile of weeds, she repeats to Brian, "Forget the hoe and help me pick up these weeds."

"Get these weeds here, Brian," she says annoyed, then adds, "Is your mother working?"

"Oh, yes, ma'am," he answers with despair. Quietly, he adds, "She always works." He then begins picking up the weeds impassively.

"I don't know why she has to work so much? Dad, he makes good money, really good money. Ten dollars an hour; how much an hour do you make, Mrs. Jagger?

She looks blankly at him thinking, "Oh, God, how do I answer this one." Then she says to Brian, "Brian, I've been a teacher for many years."

Picking up another handful of weeds, Brian stated, "My Dad's real good at his job."

"What does he do, Brian?" Mrs. Jagger asks, seeing a way to re-channel the flow of the conversation.

"Gee, guess I'm not real sure," Brian answered, remembering that he had asked once but couldn't remember what his Dad had said. "I know it's at a recycling business."

Mrs. Jagger walked a few feet away from Brian, looking at another clump of weeds. Giving a sigh, she kneels down and begins to dig at their roots.

"I like being in the garden," Brian states. "It's fun working in the dirt. My Dad says that I should pull more weeds at the house. He's real good at pulling weeds but he never seems to have time."

Mrs. Jagger looks up to see Brian's Dad pulling in his driveway. He's in his four wheel drive truck with its over-sized tires, roll bar over the back of the cab and bush grill in the front with an electric wench. Quite a man, she thinks to herself. He's probably getting ready for another hunting trip.

His last hunting trip ended with him going to the local public park, just a block from the house, and snaring a couple of ducks with breadcrumbs. When he got home, he convinced Brian that he shot those two out of the sky at the same time with the same shot. A feat Brian still talks about to whoever will listen. Of course, Mrs. Jagger never has told Brian what her co-worker had seen that morning when she looked out her dining room window that overlooks the public park and all its ducks.

"Are we done, Mrs. Jagger?" He asks, then said, "My Dad's home and I need to go."

"Sure, Brian, go ahead," she replies. "I'm done for today."

She knows that Brian will be excited to see his Dad. She also knows that Dad will assign Brian a task that will keep his son from underfoot. Brian will be ignored for the rest of the afternoon, then sent to bed early tonight.

Brian is running out of the yard now, yelling hellos to his father, telling him about his day in school. Brian's father is busy unpacking the food for the hunting trip. He looks up and says,

"Yeah, great. Brian! Grab that bag by the wheel. And, quit talking so much! You're giving me a headache."

"But, Dad, I was telling you about my test and how I finally passed," he entreats his father. "Please, Dad, listen. I got a passing grade."

"That's great," Brian's Dad responds indifferently. "Get that bag into the kitchen, NOW!"

Into the kitchen the two go as Mrs. Jagger watches and listens. Brian holding the heavy bag as he keeps the door open for Dad, then he follows. He asks, "Dad, what do you do at work, anyway?"

"What do I do at work?" his father questions. "What do you mean, what do I do?" He mincingly looks at Brian and answers, "I work, God Damn-it, I work!"

He sets down the box of groceries he has carried in, then twirls, and grabs the bag from Brian. "Brian, since you like to help the neighbor lady so much, get your ass out into our yard and pull some of our weeds."

"Hey, that's a great idea, Dad," Brian says, deciding not to ask any more questions about work.

"Where's the new hoe?" Brian asks.

"How the hell do I know," his Dad yells, adding, "I'll kick your ass if you have lost that new hoe."

Brian knows he better get out the door quickly. His Dad's temper is beginning to show.

"I know where it is, Dad," he adds quickly. "I'll find it."

"You better had, boy," his Dad, sputters. "You better had!"

Once out in the back yard Brian begins to look for the hoe. The grass is long, the weeds are longer and if anything is lying on the ground, it is hidden in the undergrowth. As he is looking for the new hoe, he spies Mrs. Jagger in her own yard still cultivating and smoothing the soil.

"Hey, Mrs. Jagger, what'cha do' in?" Brian calls out hastily. "I can help."

He leaps the small fence once again and is standing next to the picket fence before Mrs. Jagger can answer him.

Brian, looks over his shoulder towards his house, and says, "I'm really good at helping. My Dad thinks I weed the fastest. I'll get our hoe."

"Brian, no," Mrs. Jagger smiles, "you need to go back to your yard and weed. Your Dad won't be happy with you over here, helping me."

"Oh, he won't mind," Brian, responds. "My Dad likes it when I'm busy." He stands anxiously at the fence, expectantly, waiting for her to say it is all right for him to stay and help.

Mrs. Jagger thinks for a moment, then asked, "Don't you need to weed your garden? Isn't that what I heard your Dad just say to do?"

"Yeah, but I can get that done later," He answers, embarrassed that Mrs. Jagger must have heard his Dad yell. "I'll get the hoe and come help you."

And, as he races to fetch the hoe he suddenly remembers, "Gunner, here I come, boy!"

At the same moment Brian is letting Gunner out of his pen, he hears his mother drive in and honk.

"Brian," she yells! "Brian!"

"Yeah, Mom! I'm in the back getting Gunner," he yells back. He finishes filling Gunner's empty water dish. "Sorry, boy, I should've filled it this morning when I put you in." The dog ignores Brian as he takes his fill of water.

"Brian!" his mom yells once more. "Get out here and carry this shit in. Hurry!"

"OK, mom! I'm on my way," he replies loudly, then adds quietly to himself, "Get a grip."

Around the house, he races with Gunner galloping and barking alongside of him. Gunner's pink tongue is dangling out the side of his mouth as he sputters his barks, running with his young master to the front yard. Mom needs help and Brian, with Gunner, is going to the rescue.

"Get your butt over here," Brian's mother commands as soon as he and the dog come around the edge of the house.

"Get these groceries in the house, NOW." Mrs. Jagger could not help but notice the tone of the voice, shaking her head in amazement.

Brian could not contain his excitement. Someone needed him; not just someone, his mom needs him. "Coming, Mom, coming," he ran excitedly to the car as she was getting out. She practically knocked him over.

"I'll help you put them away," he said, gasping for air. Gunner barked with excitement, sure there was a surprise for him in one of those bags.

"Mom, I've got it. Let go," he commands, wanting to do the best job possible to please his mother.

"Well, hurry. I've got to get to work," she said impatiently.

Her years of work showed around the corners of her eyes in the form of creases that formed like crow's feet. Her lids were droopy and purple bags hung below her gray, hollow eyes. In the whites of her eyes was a trace of yellow. The many years of drinking are beginning to show.

"Hurry the hell up," she screams impatiently. "I ain't got all firkin day."

Brian loads up all the bags he can, unintentionally squeezes the bread, and having bad luck, drops the bag with eggs. He picks it up, pushes Gunner out of the way and then hustles into the house.

As he set the bags on the counter, he says, "Mom, I got a "B" on my math test."

She replied, "What the hell's that got to do with me going to work?" She stood there a moment as if expecting a reply.

"Mom, I said, I'll put the groceries away," he replied as he started to put the groceries in their proper places. He looked out of the corner of his eye to see if she would at least look at his test paper he had set on the counter.

It's important to him, but she is busy putting some of the groceries away, then stops suddenly, looking at her watch, saying, "I've got to go. Damn. Damn. Damn it!" Quickly she grabs her purse and coat then headed towards the door.

"Mom, did you see my test paper? Got a "B"," he calls hastily. "It's a good score, for me."

"Yeah, great Brian," she said as she disappeared through the door and out into the yard.

"I'm leaving," she yelled to her husband who was busy loading his hunting gear into his pickup.

Brian was alone in the kitchen. He could hear its silence and feel its loneliness closing in on him. He looked at the canned goods on the counter his mom hadn't the time to put away. He looked at his test paper, with its "B" in red at the top and the words, "Good job, Brian."

Suddenly, Brian is morose and gloomy. An unfathomable feeling of depression sweeps over him as he looks in the drawer. He fumbles through the utensils but he cannot find the one he wants.

Thinking to himself, maybe this is not such a great idea. Besides, he promised mom he would finish putting the groceries away.

He starts to close the drawer and as it closed, he sees it. He reaches in, grabs the serrated-edged knife, and pulls it out of the drawer.

With one swift motion, he cuts into his left wrist, just a couple of inches above the scar from the previous attempt.

He feels not the physical pain of the gash but, rather, the emotional pain that isolates and diminishes him. As the blood spurts out, he slides to the floor to quietly wait.

As darkness settled in, he feels the need for his mother and in a hushed voice, Brian simply begs, "Mom, please ..." Then he becomes very still. The blood spreads in a glossy red patch. Outside, a sparrow's song is heard, but in the kitchen, only silence.

Mrs. Jagger finishes her weeding, Brian's mother goes to work, Brian's Dad goes hunting, and Gunner scratches at the backdoor in earnest.

Acknowledgment

First and foremost, I want to thank my wife Linda whom for the past twenty years has endured a lot of my crazy ideas with patience. And, I suspect with a bit of humor. Her review and comments on this book helped me to be a better author.

Second, I want to take a moment to acknowledge an old high school buddy with whom I experienced all the challenging high school years. Roger Cannon edited all the stories in this collection of short stories with a capacity of endurance and patience. His English teacher's tolerance must have been sorely tested, but he always found a way to nicely show me the errors of my ways. Of course, his editing of my works might be the reason he has taken on an extended hike through the Pyrenees. I wish him the best on his walk along the El Camino de Santiago. Many Blessings!

Last, I want to thank Kristin Calhoun Davie for the picture of the author. Kristin is an up and coming star in the photo world that has the natural ability to rival the incomparable Ann Geddes. She presently operates KD Portraiture, doing professional photography for businesses and weddings in Yakima, Washington.

Thomas William Irons, 2014

Made in the USA
Charleston, SC
26 November 2014